THE GIFT

THE GIFT

PETE HAMILL

RANDOM HOUSE   NEW YORK

Library of Congress Cataloging in Publication Data
Hamill, Pete, 1935-
The gift.
I. Title.
PZ4.H216Gi [PS3558.A423]   813'.5'4   73-3981
ISBN 0-394-47338-8

Grateful acknowledgment is made to the following for permission to
reprint lyrics:

Page 7   Shapiro, Bernstein & Co., Inc.: Lyrics from "Red Sails in the
          Sunset," by Jimmy Kennedy. Copyright 1935 by Peter Music
          Co., Ltd. (London, England). Copyright assigned for U.S.
          and Canada and renewed to Shapiro, Bernstein & Co., Inc.
          (New York). Used by permission.

Pages   Lyrics from "Maybe." Words by Allan Flynn, music by
52, 53   Frank Madden. Copyright 1923 and renewed 1950 by Rob-
          bins Music Corp. Used by permission.

Page 54   Lyrics from "I Understand," by Kim Gannon and Mabel
          Wayne. Copyright 1941 by Leo Feist, Inc. Copyright renewal
          1969, United Artists Music Co., Inc., and Ivan Mogull Music
          Corp., N.Y., N.Y. Used by permission.

Page 66   Lyrics from "My Foolish Heart," copyright 1949 by Anne-
          Rachel Music Corporation. Used by permission.

Manufactured in the United States of America
Design by Bernard Klein
First Edition

For Shirley

I came here to sing,
and for you to sing with me.
PABLO NERUDA

1. I: him: that young man, standing there in the cold, the pea-jacket collar pulled high against the bald neck, the hat cocked saltily over the eye, the sea bag frosted with rain: that young man, seventeen years and six months old, out there at the entrance to the Jersey Turnpike, the world hammered flat and cold by the rain, a world empty of light, the tar of the road glistening and slick. I: him: five-foot-eleven, one hundred and sixty-seven pounds, chin tucked down like the fighters in the gym at home, wishing his shoulders weren't so blocky and square, wishing they sloped more, like Paddy Young's, staring out into the emptiness, watching the car lights grow from double tackholes in the dark to blurred sheets fretted with rain, the drivers stopped for the toll, paying it, and then moving on, snug containers of warmth, heading for New York, while he waited with the large man in the raincoat, under the entrance, in custody, and not caring, and thinking of steam. I: him: that young man who once was me, so strange now and distant, heading home, after a long time away.

It began somewhere else, in some other year, in a place thick with steam. I was sure of that. I slept on a couch in an aunt's house in Bay Ridge, eight years old, and it was the first time I had ever seen a radiator. The steam sprayed itself upon the windows in the deep winter night, and when I awoke, I thought it was the snow come at last, the White Christmas that Bing Crosby had promised, or the Christmas of horse-drawn sleighs, trees with serrated bark, children with heavy wool mufflers bundled against the cold, and all the fine-drawn English faces I had seen in the dank-smelling bound volumes of the *St. Nicholas* magazine in the public library on Ninth Street. But mine was no greeting-card Christmas, and there was no snow; only steam, forced from the radiator, glazing the window of that strange house, like

3

the breath of an old and very fat man. Standing on the Jersey Turnpike, I remembered that Christmas, my mother gone to the hospital, and no word from my father, no touch of his rough beard, his slick black hair, his hoarse voice.

"It should be along any minute now, sailor," the trooper said.

"You think I can get on it?" I said. "It might be crowded."

"I'll *put* you on it, young man."

The windows of the tollbooth were opaque with steam, and I remember wondering how many hours the man inside had actually worked, and whether he lived nearby, and how much he was paid. He was a fat, sloppy man, furiously smoking Camels, and looking at a Philadelphia *Bulletin*. I didn't like him. The cop was all right; he was doing his job, and part of his job was to stop people from hitchhiking on the Jersey Turnpike. But the fat guy in the booth was cloaked in steam, reading the paper, and chain-smoking his weeds, and I made him for a guy who cut his toenails and left the parings on the floor. I wondered if they had linoleum on the floors in Jersey and whether the guy had lived his whole life with steam heat.

"You comin' up from Bainbridge, son?" the trooper said.

"Yeah."

"During the war—the big war, the *last* war—most of the kids around here went up to that Great Lakes. I had a buddy went there, matter of fact. Up near Chicago. Bainbridge, that was later. You like it?"

"It's all right," I said.

"Watch your ass in that Korea."

The man in the booth leaned back, and the headline in the paper said MARINES BATTLE REDS AT CHOSIN.

"Hey," the trooper said. "Here it comes now."

Away off, two saucer-shaped lights were approaching in the darkness. The Greyhound panted up to the tollbooth, wheezing and protesting, smelling of hot rubber and burnt gasoline. The windshield wipers slapped away rain as the trooper waved and the doors opened. The guy in the tollbooth nodded, and went back to his paper.

"I got one for you, Jerry," the trooper said.

"No problem," the driver said.

I shouldered the sea bag and moved to the door.

"Try not to hitchhike on the turnpike again, sailor. It's only a mess of trouble."

"Yeah."

I started to get on, and the trooper touched my arm. "You got enough money, son?"

I looked at him: he had a kind face, and I liked him. "Enough."

I stepped on, but when I turned to tell him thanks, the trooper was gone.

2.
The Greyhound roared up the turnpike in the rain, as I lurched down the aisle, afraid of slamming someone with the sea bag, my eyes raw to the dark. A small red light burned at the back of the bus, vague and fogged, and I could smell stale tobacco smoke and wet wool. Something soft moved under my foot: a guy sprawled out, sleeping on a duffel bag; he moved, but did not awake, and then I was able to see. The bus was filled with servicemen: sailors up from Bainbridge, dressed like me in blues and white hats;

soldiers from the South, with their caps tucked in the shirt flaps; and above us, luggage racks groaning with sea bags and duffel bags. They were all going on Christmas leave, in the winter of Korea, the last turn home for most of them. I: him: that young man among them, sliding now into an empty seat, tired, feeling the fierce power of the bus as it left the cars behind, the thick wheels ripping through the cold shallow ponds of water along the highway: I leaned back and tried to sleep.

"Smoke?"

It was the guy next to me: Army, dark-haired, one-stripe, hard-faced: handing me a pack of Camels, with a butt sliding out like a bullet.

"Thanks," I said.

"Where you comin' from, that Bainbridge?"

"Yeah. Christmas leave, you know . . ."

"Me too. Some friggin' weather, ain't it?"

"Yeah."

He stuck out his hand, I shook it, and we introduced ourselves. His name was Sal Costella, from the Bronx.

"How long you been away?" he said.

"Since Labor Day. What about you?"

"Sixteen weeks. Sixteen weeks of shit-kickin' music, sixteen weeks of marchin', guard duty, sergeants, shit on a shingle . . . 'Ey, they got that shit on a shingle in the Navy, or what?"

"Yeah," I said. "Twice a week."

"Isn't that the most disgusting friggin' thing you ever friggin' ate?"

"It's right up there, Sal."

"Jesus, I'd rather be in that Korea, I swear to God, with the Chinese blowin' their bugles, and eatin' C-rations than eat that shit on a shingle. I mean, what *is* that friggin' stuff anyway?"

"It's creamed chipped beef."

"Yeah. But what is *creamed chipped beef*?"

"Jesus, I don't know."

"I mean what kind of an animal does it come off of? One of them cows? Or a pig? Or a veal? Or what?"

"There's an animal called a veal?"

"There gotta be."

"I mean a cow, a pig, a horse even, but a veal?"

"Well, who ever head of *beef* cutlet Parmesan, or *pork* cutlet Parmesan?"

"Yeah, I see what you mean."

"There gotta be an animal called a veal."

He lit himself another cigarette. In the back of the bus, four paratroopers were singing; they were good.

> *"Red sails in the sunset,*
> *Way out on the sea,*
> *Please carry my lover,*
> *home safely to me . . ."*

There was movement in the bus, as the sad, hushed words of the song drifted among the young men. Sal stared out the window for a long while. Small rivers of rain were running down the glass. When the song ended, he seemed to shake himself into brightness.

"Hey, are you a Dodger fan?"

"Yeah."

"Aaah, well."

He seemed disappointed, as if he had just learned that I belonged to some strange and secret religion.

"You're a Giant fan, right?"

"Look," he said brightly. "It don't really matter, right? I mean, we're bot' from New York, right. I mean, they got guys in the Army from St. Louis! From *Saint Louis*!"

He was stunned and astonished: the world had people
in it from everywhere, from Jersey and Maine and Con-
necticut, and even from St. Louis, where Stan Musial played
all season long and Enos Slaughter hit them over the pavil-
ion roof. And I thought about the first week in boot camp,
the strange handled feeling I had, as I was pushed through
tests, scalped in the barbershop, shoved through lines of
dentists who scoured and yanked the soft Irish teeth; all in
a cold place with strange accents and long bony hillbilly
faces, and how that week I realized for the first time that the
Navy was going to be a place where things were done to me.

"You gotta girl?" Sal said, almost gently.

"I think so."

"Uh, oh. One a those, huh?"

Maybe. But where I came from you didn't talk much
about your girls; it was as if the edge of the precipice was
always too near: a false roll, a rumble of doubt, and off you
would go, falling into the darkness. And so, rolling through
the Jersey night, I said nothing; instead, I tried to conjure
her face. Her picture was in the wallet tucked into the Navy
blues, but I didn't take it out. I had studied the picture too
often: every night, standing guard over garbage cans, drifting around the frozen boundaries of the base, staring up
from the picture to the Maryland sky, forming her with
memory, trying to remember precisely how she smelled, what
her hair felt like, what it was like to touch her lean flesh.

The paratroopers were singing "You Belong to Me"
now, all about the pyramids along the Nile, and the jungle
when it's wet with rain, and I remembered the V.F.W. post
down near the Venus movie house, the night I had gone
away; Mousey and Joe Kelly and a lot of the guys, all sloppy
with beer, the floor a dense mash of pretzels and spilled
drinks, and then someone hit Joe Griffin from the Gremlins,

and one of the Gremlins hit Tommy Conroy: until all of us were fighting in the sloppy mash, sprawling and violent, with glasses breaking and the girls screaming and Jo Stafford singing. I knocked down two people with punches, and my right hand was skinned, and I was going to hit Eddie Norris when I saw Kathleen going out the door. She was crying, and I remembered the way her hair bobbed when she moved, dressed in a tight-fitting wine-colored coat, hurrying away from the violence, the broken glass, and me. And then I was behind her, running after her in the damp September night, rushing along Seeley Street, feeling thick and sodden and clumsy. Until I caught her, and held her hand, and hugged her to me; telling her I loved her, pouring it out of myself, all the desire, need, all the jammed-up pain and loneliness of that summer when I had tried to make myself clear to her. I told her that I was only going away for a while, but not forever. It was the best thing for me, for her, for us; I could finish high school in the Navy, pick up a craft, maybe get a job drawing cartoons for the base paper, something like that, something that would let me learn and shine. And her body tensed as I held her, and I realized that she was afraid.

And now on the bus I tried again to remember her with precision, the texture of her skin, the angle of her teeth: but she remained trapped in the image of the cracked photograph in the wallet, a thin girl with a sad wry face, wearing the long wine-colored coat, sitting at the end of a row of benches which wound around a path in Prospect Park, in the direction of Monument Hill. That was what I had ended up with at the end of the three months in boot camp: a face in a photograph, to which I tried to match the neat, precise Catholic girl's school handwriting. Not much else. The darkness of the bus was punctuated by struck matches and bright washes of light from passing cars, and I stared out at the rain-glossy roads, past the small neat towns and the clumps of dark forest, out past the neon of roadside taverns, past the blue-white glare of gas stations and the bright wilderness of those early 1952 shopping centers, to the place where Kathleen lived, getting there at sixty miles an hour. I was listening for her voice and the sound of her laughter and trying to control what was happening in my stomach as I fought off the anxious knowledge that she might no longer be there.

"They got many hoowiz around Bainbridge?" Sal said. He was from New York all right; he pronounced "whores" *hoowiz* and I loved the way it sounded.

"Yeah. Pretty ugly though. Down in that East Baltimore Street in Baltimore. They got them up the ass."

"I don't understand hoowiz," he said. "I mean, how could they just lay there and let all them guys stick it in them like that, night afta night? They must feel like a pincushion."

"I don't know. They must like it."

"Tell ya the truth I bet they don't. Somebody told me one time that most of them was, uh, Lesbians. You know, lady fags."

"You really think so?"

"I don't know. I mean I can't see payin' for it anyway, can you?"

"There was a guy I knew in camp who said to me once, 'A load in the hand is worth a gallon in the balls.' "

"Yeah, but you don't get the clap offa your hand." He started to laugh. And I remembered the third floor in the Federal Hotel, the blood-red color of the Neapolitan sunset on the wall over the bed, and the woman's black garters digging into her thighs, and her silky black patch; her hands

soapy and warm and giving; the one gray tooth in the
mouth, and the gray dead flesh around the hips; and how she
touched me, soft, kneading, as I kissed the dark brown
nipples, the ashtray beside the bed filled with other people's
cigarette butts, all tongue, handkerchief, hand, hair, with
the Four Roses for courage, and spreading and wetness and
entry; until I suddenly thought of my mother, who was the
same age of this woman stranger. And felt panic and fear
scribble through me, and tried to drive the face away, with
its soft memory of powder and flesh in the darkness. *We
lived in Madrid Street and my father had red hair,* until it
was finished. Lying under the Neapolitan sunset, forcing
down the Four Roses, the paint green and flaking, the rug
an impacted gray mat, I stared at the uniform hanging over
the straight-backed chair, the mingled sounds of East Baltimore Street drifting in through the window, wondering if
she would steal the wallet. Instead, she talked softly, con-
solingly, fondly almost, touching the rope burn on my back
that I got in the gym at the base, washing, kneading me
again, until she wrapped her large body around me, en-
veloping me, holding me flat, until I slept. I: him: that young
man, sitting in the bus, dreaming of teachers, trying so hard
to be a man: *just remember, darling, all the while, you belong
to me.*

I moved deeper into the seat, thinking about the last
hour with Kathleen on the porch of the house on Seeley
Street, talking about the great cities of the world and how
I wanted to see them all, while she looked at me with puzzled
blankness; thinking about that chill night and its sense of
fracture; thinking about how I was seventeen and a half
now and on my own at last; thinking about how I was
finally becoming armored; and always, over and over, in
flashes and for long spaces, as miles rolled, and Sal Costella

slept, as the songs droned in the back of the bus, and the wheels of the bus made a tearing sound as they rolled through the rain: always thinking of her, and how I was coming home for Christmas with its promise of steam and warmth, a girl's brown hair, the smell of pine, and snow.

3. A little after one, the bus pulled up out of the tunnel, made its way into Manhattan and groaned into the Greyhound Terminal on Thirty-fourth Street.

"Oh, wow," Sal shouted, suddenly awake. He grabbed for his bag as the bus roared with movement and excitement. "Hey, good talkin' to ya. Listen, how long you gonna be home?"

"Just till the twenty-eighth."

"You mean, you're missin' New Year's?"

"Yeah."

"Well, listen, gimma ya number, we could get together."

"We don't have a phone."

"You don't have a *phone*?"

"Costs money."

"Well, listen, call *me*." He produced a pencil and started writing on a scrap torn from a newspaper. The paper said something about Ike and his cabinet, and fighting in Korea. He handed me the paper and I stuffed it in the pocket of the pea jacket. The bus stopped. "New York," the driver shouted, and the mechanical doors opened at last.

"How much do I owe you?" I asked the driver.

"Forget it, kid," he said. And turned away: maybe it was the season, but I remember the small kindness.

The bus station smelled of gasoline fumes and frying hot dogs and too many people. Sal shouldered his way out the door, into the din. Bing Crosby was singing "Blue Christmas Without You" on a jukebox. And away off to the side a knot of people exploded into life, a dark girl raced forward, heading for Sal, who fell to his knees in comic exaggeration and kissed the ground.

"New York!" he shouted, and we all laughed, and I decided that maybe I would call him later in the week. His friends were all Italian, dressed in wraparound jackets and thick-soled Flagg Bros. shoes, and what we used to call "gingerella hats"; the dark girl was first to him, and Sal hugged and squeezed her and then the rest of his crowd were on him, hoisting him into the air as if he were Audie Murphy and had just come home after capturing the whole Chinese Army. Behind them, a sad congress of colored people waited in silence for buses that would take them back to the South; several older women cried as other young men boarded buses that would take them off to the other bases, where they would be changed into soldiers and sailors and sent to Korea; a few cops, some scattered night people chewing doughnuts in the blue glare of the fluorescent lights—all of it played against the mechanical roar of engines and city noise and that jukebox playing somewhere about Christmas and absence and young men going away.

Nobody was there to meet me. I hadn't really expected anyone; in Bainbridge, we didn't know until the last minute just when we were leaving, and I wanted to hitchhike and save the money; we had no phone, of course, but even if we had, I would not have called. Three weeks earlier, Kathleen had written to me, in that almost prim handwriting, and what she said was ambiguous and fearful; the letter is gone now, but it said something about how things had changed and how I should really go on with my life in the Navy and go to see the world and how she was almost ready to graduate and would be working and how she hoped I would understand.

I had written to her, long, passionately, the letter printed rather than written longhand, because I wanted to be a cartoonist then, and I thought that was the way artists wrote letters; asking her what she meant and whether she was going to be there when I came home and how I missed her. She had not answered. And so there was a part of me that wanted to come home and surprise her, to arrive suddenly, looking mysterious, a figure from a Bogart movie, slightly world-weary and cynical, and able to endure anything. And underneath was the rest of me, scared, and crying, and wanting her. So I chose silence. She refused to answer me, and I suspended my need; I didn't write to her, and arrived alone in New York, telling myself that it did not matter. But as I stepped into that early-morning bus station, it seemed to matter more than I ever thought it would; even today, after a thousand airports, some trace of that first empty return stays with me. When I arrive somewhere late at night, a part of me always hopes that a woman will be standing in the crowd and call my name.

I went out into Thirty-fourth Street, the sea bag on my shoulder, and started walking toward Eighth Avenue to take the subway home. The rain was softening, the gloss fading from the streets. Suddenly, a drunk lurched across the wet street, dressed in an Ike jacket dyed black, and a taxi screeched to a stop in front of him.

"Dumb son of a bitch," the driver screamed.

"Ah, me," the drunk sighed. "Ah, me."

And then he spun away, like a stunned dancer, the dry wattles under his chin shaking, the back of his rummy's raw neck hunched against a blow that never came. I started to laugh. I was back in New York.

4. The A train smelled of urine and stale air, with a few people sprawled on the long seats. A Transit Authority man with a chocolate face read the *Daily News,* and a couple of cleaning women in worn wool dresses huddled together in the seat near the door. I started to get excited, because the subway was home; it was something I couldn't explain to the guys I'd met at Bainbridge, people from Lorain, Ohio, and Marietta, Georgia, and a lot of other places I'd never heard of before. They would talk about cars with souped-up V-8 engines, of roaring down dark highways at night, of the intricate codes of blinking lights and motor etiquette; they weren't mean about any of this, but they talked about it with a passion I couldn't fully understand. One of them had worked at the Fruehauf plant in Cleveland, and talked about the big long-haul trucks the way some people spoke about women. And when I tried to explain about subways they didn't understand. But the subways were a part of home to me, and I loved the sense of penetration they gave me, the roaring jamming slide into the blackness of the tunnels, the knowledge you had that you were deep below other life, that there in the tunnel you were being hurled under salesmen and millionaires, great stores and glittering mansions. I loved the charging rhythm of the train, its sense of plunge and blur, its violent race to Brooklyn.

At Jay Street-Borough Hall, I crossed the platform to the D train, waiting there for our arrival, the odd muted golden color of its incandescent lights a signal of warmth. That was our train, the one that serviced the neighborhood, the one that took the young guys to their first jobs as messengers on Wall Street, the one where you might see a familiar face. In the mornings, the young men would travel on the subway with their girls, separating at the various stops; whole engagements, marriages, and small disasters had been played out along that line; you knew there was trouble with a guy and his girl when you saw him start to travel alone, on a different train, for two or three days in a row. All summer I had met Kathleen there every morning; and once, a long time before, I had gone to a St. Patrick's Day dance in Manhattan with my mother and father, using that train, and watched the poles in the tunnel fly by: until we arrived at the dance, and my father edged over to his friends, the people who had seen him play soccer in the old days, while I sat at a table covered with pitchers of beer and later won a small contest, dancing with my mother. We came home together on the D train, and my father slept all the way.

Now, deep into the night, I didn't recognize anyone, and I looked hard at the other passengers, trying to read their faces, wondering at the same time what they thought of me; wishing they could know me and I could know them. If it had been warmer, I would have taken the pea jacket off, and rolled up the sleeves of the dress blues, where I had sewn in some garish Oriental dragons; perhaps then I would become the object of their fantasies, they would envy me my life, dream of distant places with exotic names—Rangoon and Singapore and Bali. And I thought about my grandfather, who had worked the famous merchant ships, making the run out of Liverpool in the old days, picking up cargoes of spices and silks, a first mate, tall—my mother said—and handsome; he kept his appointment on a Brooklyn dock, falling between the quay and the ship, crushed to death. *We lived in Madrid Street and my father had red hair.* I wondered about Belfast, where they all had lived before making the move to America; Belfast, where people actually seemed to care whether you were Catholic or Protestant and were prepared to kill you over the difference. I tried not to think about my father.

As the train pushed through the tunnel, making the hard metallic turn at Bergen Street and out onto the high trestle over the Gowanus Canal, I wished I had arrived earlier, that I had spent some of my $36 for the bus fare, that I had called Kathleen. Below me, the Gowanus looked like a smear of fresh tar, and the Kentile sign burned red against the sky, and off to the right, in the long slope of the hills, my slice of Brooklyn lay brooding in the darkness.

When I got out at the Seventh Avenue stop, the rain had ended. The avenue stretched before me, with a broad flat hump lying in the middle where tar covered the old trolley tracks, and the neon lights of the bars blinking their welcomes. It was cold and damp, but the avenue had its strange, comfortable sense of the familiar; even today, whenever I go back, it feels the same, as if the years we all spent there had given us permanent possession of the place. The avenue was lined with four-story tenements whose faces were marred with fire escapes: dark, hard, spiky, rectangular presences through the winter nights, and airborne areaways full of people, plants, goldfish bowls and blankets in summer. None of the houses on the avenue had backyards, so we lived on the fire escapes and the rooftops, while through the summer nights the adults sat outside on folding chairs borrowed from the funeral parlor. But on this winter night, it was deserted, and the air was still tingling with rain, a wetness so fine that it made the pea jacket glisten; there were no stars, and the avenue faded away into a blue fog; you could not see the shape of Greenwood Cemetery at the far end.

I looked into the window of Diamond's Bar and Grill on Ninth Street; my father seldom went there any more, but I thought it might be one of those late Fridays when he was traveling. There were a few old men at the far end of the dark bar, but my father wasn't there. Fitzgerald's, on the corner of Tenth Street, was a bright, high-ceilinged place, all polished wood and tile floors. It was a whiskey drinkers' bar, a place for cops and firemen and ironworkers, and before I went away I had started going there. My father didn't go there much. His bar was Rattigan's on Eleventh Street, and it was a place where I had not gone since I was twelve, when I had been stashed in a booth in the back to drink ginger ale with a maraschino cherry and consume most of a bowl of pretzels. Rattigan's was their club: the club of the older men, my father's people, the guys who had come back from World War II, the hard drinkers, the brawlers, the guys who had been, as they said, in the country for a visit. It was across the street from where we lived, and on summer evenings, the bar sounds would roar through the nights: shouting over baseball, angry arguments over politics (they were almost all Democrats there), the boisterous entrance of wives in search of husbands, fierce resistance to outsiders, and through the nights, my father's voice.

That voice, rough-edged, sometimes harsh, drifted up to me through all those summer nights while I tried to sleep in the small room with the bunk beds that I shared with my brother Tommy. The songs were always about Ireland, about Galway Bay, and the strangers who came and tried to teach us their ways; about Patty McGinty's Goat and My Old Scalara Hat and the Night That Rafferty's Pig Ran Away;

about Kevin Barry and the Bold Fenian Men, about Innisfree
and Tipperary, about Irish men fighting British guns with
pikes; songs of laughter, songs of the Green Glens of
Antrim, where he had been born, songs of young men who
had crossed oceans and chosen exile. Sometimes, in the
summer, with the whole house asleep, I would crawl out onto
the fire escape, and lie there—eight, ten, twelve, fourteen
years old—looking down and across the avenue, looking at the
Rattigan's sign hanging out over the tavern, the door open
to the night, and hear my father's voice singing there, for
strangers and friends, as year faded into year, all years the
same, singing about some long-gone green island and his
own sweet youth. Across all those summers, just once, I
wanted him to sing them to me.

And so on this night, back on the avenue and heading
for home, I wanted somehow to see him. I wanted him to see
me in my uniform, wanted to have him hug me and buy me
a drink, wanted to hear the songs. I looked into Fitzgerald's,
but didn't see him. Someone waved, and I waved back and
walked on. But the door opened behind me.

"Hey, Peter, hey! *Hamill!*"

It was a guy named Richie Brenner, one of those fine
thick beer-drinking Irishmen who didn't care how old anyone happened to be as long as the anyone could drink. He
worked at the Rheingold Brewery and was as strong as a
door. I always liked him because the strength and bulk were
wrapped around a kind man.

"Hey, wodja, just get back?"

"Yeah, Richie. How've ya been?"

"Sensational. Come on in. Have a jar."

"Jesus, Richie, I'd love to but, you know, it's late
and . . ."

"Come on."

He had his hand around my shoulder and was pushing
me through the doors; the sea bag tottered and he grabbed
it and went in carrying it. I had no choice.

"Two Dewars."

"Hey, Richie, just a beer, I . . ."

"Whiskey. You been away, you gotta have whiskey. And
the *best* whiskey. Not that bear piss, that Four Roses and
crap like that."

The bartender pulled a couple of beers, and poured the
whiskeys into shot glasses beside them: it was called compro-
mise. There was a knot of firemen at the far end of the bar,
talking to a guy they called Vinnie Victory, because he got
drunk on V-J day and stayed drunk for four years. Vinnie
Victory was singing "Stardust." He couldn't sing.

"You seen my old man, Richie?"

"He was in earlier. He was feelin' no pain, I'll tell ya
that."

"Stewed?"

"A pretty good package. But don't worry. He was okay,
everything was copacetic."

"Whatta you mean?"

I didn't like the taste of the whiskey, so I threw it down
fast and chased it with the beer.

"Ah, you know how he gets."

"Yeah."

"You know, someone starts to break his balls and he
breaks their balls back, and it's always a possibility. I mean,
he hit some guy in Rattigan's a month ago, some young guy,
and knocked the guy under the shuffleboard. He's hot shit
all right."

"Yeah."

I finished the beer and put a five-dollar bill on the bar.

"Let's have another round," I said to the bartender.

Nobody could go home in that neighborhood if someone else
had bought the last round; it made for late nights.

"Get adda here," Brenner said. "You just got *home,*
your money ain't worth nothin' here."

And so I had three drinks, while Brenner went on about
the Dodgers, Eisenhower, the bastards at his plant, that
goddamn Truman, Bill O'Dwyer, and the guineas. In that
neighborhood, it always came around to the guineas, which
is what they called the Italians. They were lowbred, treach-
erous, oversexed, criminal bastards. Almost everybody was
sure of that. If you fought them, watch out for knives and
guns. And if you had a sister, watch out for them, period.
Brenner was convinced that if the Italians and the Communists would only get on the boat together and go back
where they came from, everything would be all right. He
said all this with great laughter, amusement and energy,
but after a while, I said good night, picked up the sea bag
and started home.

I crossed the street and walked past Rattigan's. It was a
dark place, with low lights, and a Schlitz sign bubbling over
the cash register. I looked in over the curtain rod, but didn't
see Billy Hamill. Someone waved, and I waved back and
crossed the street to go home. I looked up and the windows
were white with steam.

5. The house was at 378 Seventh Avenue. There was
a small butcher shop to the left and Teddy's Sandwich Shop
to the right, and when I went in, I saw that the mailbox was
still broken and the hall smelled of backed-up sewers and

wet garbage. There were, of course, no locks on the doors, and I stood for a while in the yellow light of the thirty-watt bulb, and shifted the sea bag to the other shoulder. Two baby carriages were parked beside the stairs, and in the blackness at the back of the hall, I caught a glimpse of battered garbage cans. A small shudder went through me; the back of that hall had always been a fearful place when I was small, a place where I always felt vulnerable: to sudden attacks from the open door leading to the cellar, to rats feasting on the wet garbage, to unnamed things, specters, icy hands, the vengeance of God. Once, I'd had to go to the cellar late at night. To the right, inside the cellar door, there was a light switch, covered with a ceramic knob. I reached for the knob and it was gone, and there was a raw wire there instead and the shock knocked me over backwards, into the garbage cans, my heart spinning and racing away, and then rushing back again. I thought of that night trip, the strangeness later when I realized for the first time what it must feel like to die, and I started up the stairs.

It was a hall as familiar as anything I've ever known before or since. First floor right, Mae McAvoy; on the left, Poppa Clark; second floor right, Anne Sharkey and Mae Irwin; left, Carrie Woods. Carrie was a tiny sparrow of a woman who kept dogs and drank whiskey, and the dogs started a ferocious attack on the locked door, trying to get at me—alarmed, I suppose, by a smell they had not sensed for many weeks. All the apartments had the feeling of tossing bodies within, and I remembered fragments of other nights: the scream when a husband punched out a wife, and how he left and never came back; the glasses breaking at some forgotten party and the blood in the hall later; how they all hated one of the women because she was a wine drinker and therefore a snob; the great large silent man in

one of those apartments, who played each Christmas with a
vast Lionel electric train set, while forcing his only daughter
to play at an untuned upright piano, who rooted for the
Giants in that neighborhood of Dodger fans, and who had a
strange tortured set of eyes. At each landing there were
sealed metal doors where the dumbwaiter once had been, a
pit that dropped away, like some bottomless well, to a
boarded-over access door in the cellar, and which I thought,
when I was eight, was the way to Hell itself, or at the very
least, to the secret cave where Shazam granted Billy Batson
the magic powers. There were two more baby carriages at
the top of the second floor, the floor where my father had so
often stopped on his way home, emptied of songs, dry and
hoarse, unable to make that one final flight of stairs to bed.
Billy Batson. Billy Hamill. Shazam.

There were traces of dinner smells in the hall, as if you
could chew the air itself. It was almost three.

The door to our apartment was not locked. I dropped
the sea bag, pushed the door open easily, and stepped into
the dark kitchen, groping for the light cord in the center of
the room. I bumped into a chair, then the table, and then
found the light cord. A transformer hummed for a few
seconds and then the round fluorescent ceiling light blinked
on. The room was as I had remembered it: a white-topped
gas range against the far wall where the old coal stove had
once stood, a tall white cabinet to the left, and then the sink,
high, one side shallow and the other deep, next to the window
that never opened. A Servel refrigerator with a broken
handle was next to the bathroom door. A closet loomed behind me next to the front door, with a curtain covering the
disorder within, and there was a table in the center of the
room, linoleum on the floor, and a clothesline running the
length of the room because there was no backyard, and in

winter the clothes froze on the line on the roof. There was
a picture of Franklin Roosevelt on one wall, a map of Ireland
from the *Daily News* on another, and beside it I saw some
of the drawings I had sent from boot camp. Some of them
were cartoons, drawings of soldiers and pilots I had copied
from Milton Caniff; the others were something new, drawings of sailors' faces, done in ink washes, the first drawings
I had made that didn't look like comic-strip figures. Roaches
scurried across the table, panicked by the harshness of the
sudden blue-tinged light. I could hear movement at the other
end of the railroad flat, the smell of heavy breathing and
milk, and then my mother was coming through the rooms.

"Oh, Peter," she said. "You're home."

And she hugged me.

6.

The kitchen was suddenly alive with a muffled busy-
ness: the teakettle filled with water, toast placed on the bottom of the oven, butter and sugar and milk laid out on the
table, all of it accomplished with no clatter of dish against
table, or metal against metal. She was wearing a faded blue
flannel robe, buttoned down the front, and I realized how
small she was; maybe five-three at best; and also how she
was finally getting old. I remembered her when we lived in
the other house on Fourteenth Street, with silky brown hair
cut in a twenties bob, and the way she moved around all the
time, trying to catch up with the cleaning, trying to cook
as more and more children arrived, and how I loved to hear
her whistle. When she was whistling, life among us was

going well; it was the bleak dark silences I feared, evenings
when she sat alone in the kitchen, writing to her brother,
who still lived in Belfast, reading books by A. J. Cronin,
sipping tea, or finally, alone.

Fourteenth Street had been the best time, with the snow
piling up on the window sills in winter, and long walks in
the evening through the deep green glades of Prospect Park.
She told me once about a ride she took on a horse, when she
was a little girl in Ireland. "I rode and rode, and didn't know
how to make the horse move," she said. "It kept flying across
meadows and streams, into woods, and I had never been on a
horse before, and didn't know how to make it stop. Until I
screamed, and panicked, and fell off. I was almost killed and
never rode a horse again." She told me all that in the park,
as we walked in the Big Meadow, near the bridle path, where
the red chestnut horses would trot in the afternoons. That
was during the time of the other house: so was the night we
went to see *The Wizard of Oz* at the Sanders, she and I,
watching its wonders, tornadoes, tin men who talked and
lions who were afraid; and later, darkness around us, skip-
ping home together, with me holding her hand. I was five
then.

"Was it terrible?" she said now.

"Come on, Mom. It was only boot camp."

"I know, son. But the papers are full of this stupid war
and, well, mothers do have a right to worry."

Yes. And then I started school, in the big Catholic place
on the hill, a place of rowdy terror, wild children, seventy-
two of them in the wartime class. We moved to another place
farther down the hill, away from the deep green glade of the
park, to a street where no trees lived, and a backyard was
made of mud. We spent two years there. My brother Tommy

and my sister Kathleen at home, and my father working nights: only five of us: and yet I was never alone with her. At night I wanted to sleep with her, to slide in beside her, feel her arms around me, smother with her warmth. I started to read instead.

"The Navy's there too, isn't it? In Korea?"

"They have a lot of ships there, but it's no danger."

"There's always danger, especially on a ship."

"I'll probably end up in North Africa anyway."

"North Africa? Who ever heard of a sailor in North Africa?"

"They have a place there called Port-Lyautey. It's some kind of a fueling station. I put in for it."

I rolled up my sleeves, to show the elaborate dragons sewn into the cuffs. She didn't notice.

"Mickey Watson's dead."

"No kidding."

"On his way home from Mass, and just dropped dead. Only fifty-three."

"He was a nice man."

"He was."

I remembered him once on the beach at Coney, with the Irish crowd all camped on blankets in front of Scoville's. My father was up at the bar. My mother, Anne Hamill, sat alone, staring at the sea, and Mickey Watson, red and peeling from the sun, brought me a soda. He didn't say anything; he just handed it to me, as if I were a man and he were handing me a beer. And then he went down to the shore and I watched him climb out on the rocks of the breakwater, and sit alone, staring away at the flat edge of the world, while swimmers bobbed in the water around him. He had never married.

She poured the tea, steaming and brilliant. I added milk from the bottle and three sugars.

"You've gotten bigger. And heavier."

"They march you around a lot. It makes you hungry as hell."

Remembering hunger: bread and butter covered with sugar in the afternoons home from school. She worked from one to five thirty at the RKO Prospect, selling tickets, and the afternoons were a yawning emptiness. The radio was filled with soap operas, "Portia Faces Life," "Lum 'n' Abner," a lot of others I can't remember. There was one about a newspaperman called "Front-Page Farrell," but the plots were too complicated and I didn't understand it. If the weather was all right, I played in the streets—stickball, box-ball, ringolevio, all the other New York games. But in the heavy rains, I retreated into the comic books, into Captain America and Captain Marvel, the Boy Commandoes, Batman, Ibis the Invincible. They were the world to me; I flew over buildings; small and defenseless, I too said, "Shazam," and went out to fight evil. When I was eleven I started drawing my own comics, all about a pilot I called Smilin' Jack, but who bore no resemblance to the character in the *Daily News*; my guy fought someone named the Red Bat, fought him in caves and jungles and islands, on rafts tossed by rivers, but never in cities. I started collecting them, buying used comics in a store on Sixth Avenue, trading them with other kids; the buzzer would ring, "Wanna trade?" would echo up the hall, and the deals would be made. But that was my life. My father wasn't there; he was out at the Arma plant in Bush Terminal, working nights all through the war, sleeping days, and a voice on summer weekends drifting up from the bar, the sad, gay song of a man I did not know.

"Where's he?" I said.

"Oh, sleeping . . ."

There was a flicker of concealment in her voice; the toast was too well done, and she rasped off some of the blackened crust with a knife.

"Sleeping one off, you mean."

"Ah, he waited up for a while, Peter. I mean, we thought you'd be here today or tomorrow, we just weren't sure, Peter. He does have to work tomorrow, the overtime—"

"I wish we had a phone."

"It's a twenty-five-dollar deposit . . ."

"I know."

I finished the tea, and she lifted the cup. I wanted to talk to her, but didn't know how to start.

"I'm sorry, Peter, all I've got for you is the couch."

"Ah, don't worry, Mom," I said, rising from the table, but not looking at her. "It's home."

I walked through the rooms, past the sleeping children: Tommy, fifteen and small, Brian, who was six, Johnny, four, Denis, two. My sister Kathleen was twelve now, and had taken possession of the only room with a door. I passed my father's bed. He was there asleep, the breathing thick, and the room sour with the smell of beer. I undressed in the dark, and stood for a while in my underclothes, moving aside the shade. The window was fogged, and I drew a face with my finger in the steam. Through one of the eyes, I could see the red light of Rattigan's sign, a half-hour from closing time.

I slid under the blanket and lay there, listening to the familiar dense sounds of home: forms breathing in the darkness, someone's dry cough, the heavy wheezing of the buses on the street below, and the radiator's thin hiss. Everywhere we had lived it had been coal stoves and kerosene heaters, until three years earlier when we got steam heat. I couldn't

believe it. Steam heat was something my aunts and uncles
and cousins had out in Bay Ridge, something people had who
lived in the brownstones up on the hill. Down there, on
Seventh Avenue, it was walk-ups and cold-water flats; or
coal stoves and hot water, but no steam. And here it was,
three years later, still throwing heat around the packed
apartment. And after a while I realized that the light was
still on in the kitchen, that there was no sound of dishes
being washed. My mother was still there. I looked out
through the rooms, and she was sitting alone. Her back was
to me. I started to doze, drifting into a memory of garters
and flesh, until a fire engine banged me awake. I thought
again about Kathleen, and how difficult it would be in the
morning, the uneasiness gnawing at me, thinking about her
face being touched by another man's hand, imagining her
later with gray hair, wondering about her naked, wanting
her beside me, then driving the thoughts away, driving away
visions of white flesh moving naked through rooms, pushing
it away, uneasy still, and sometime near dawn I fell asleep.

7. I awoke to a room flooded with an oblique winter
sun. The blanket was pink wool, and itchy, except on the
edges, where it was trimmed with sateen. I was used to the
broad ceiling beams of barracks, open rows of bunk beds,
the wide chill murmur of boot-camp mornings. Now I was
in a room that had once been large and suddenly had shrunk,
and my eyes played on the lone picture, two snow-white parrots in a Brazilian jungle.

The jungle had to be Brazil; I had figured that out one

time in geography class, and I was probably wrong. But I
knew that parrots had to mean South America, because they
didn't have them in Africa. And lying there, gradually becoming familiar, with the molding around the ceiling trim-
ming the green walls, feeling safe, I thought of Bomba. *A
jagged streak of lightning shot athwart the sky, followed
by a deafening crash of thunder. The lurid glare revealed
Bomba, the jungle boy, crouched in a hollow beneath the
roots of an overturned tree.* It was from "Bomba the Jungle
Boy in the Swamp of Death, or The Sacred Alligators of
Abarago" by Roy Rockwood, and I had memorized those
opening lines, sitting alone at the top of the stairs one
summer, next to the roof door. Bomba lived in a South
American jungle with a naturalist named Cody Casson; he
didn't know his mother or father, and reading about him,
about how old Casson had been injured in an accident, and
how Bomba became the provider, how at fourteen he was as
strong as men twice his age, I would inhabit that distant
jungle, alone, fighting pumas, jaguars, snakes, storms and
cannibals. I copied pictures out of the books, which were
published by Cupples and Leon, and which my brother
Tommy and I would buy in the used-book store on Pearl
Street, and once, with a flat sheet of cork stolen from a factory, I carved a whole river system, marked with jungles,
native villages, and the massive headwaters of the Giant
Cataract. At the end of every book, Bomba got closer to dis-
covering the secret of his vanished parents, whose names
were Andrew and Laura Bartow, and I wandered the used-
book shops trying to find the missing volumes in the series,
the volumes that would tell the whole story about this white
boy lost in the South American jungle. Each book would end
with Bomba wondering about his mother, longing for her,
crying alone in the jungle. I never did find the missing
volumes.

I looked up and my brother Denis was staring at me. He was only two, a kid with square shoulders and huge wet brown eyes. He was standing beside a chair, tentative and puzzled.

"Hello, Denis."

He said nothing.

"Don't you remember me?"

Wordless, he turned and started to run, waddling as he went, heading for the kitchen. Everybody else was gone, including my father. I got up and went to my father's closet. An old pair of light-blue civilian trousers was hanging next to a zipper jacket. I pulled them on, then took a shirt out of his drawer. Above the bureau, brown and fading, was an old photograph of an Irish soccer team. There were fifteen players and two coaches, and there was a banner before them that said *St. Mary's*. One of the players was my father.

The year before, after dropping out of high school, I had worked for a year in the sheet-metal shop of the Brooklyn Navy Yard, and men there had told me how good my father had been, when he was young and playing soccer in the immigrant leagues. He was fierce and quick, they said, possessed of a magic leg, moving down those Sunday playing fields as if driven by the engines of anger and exile, playing hardest against English and Scottish teams, the legs pumping and cutting and stealing the ball; hearing the long deep roar of strangers, the women on the sidelines, the hard-packed earth, the ice frozen in small pools, the needle beer in metal containers, and the speak-easies later, drinking until the small hours, singing the songs they had learned across an ocean. Until one day, in one hard-played game, a German forward had come out of nowhere and kicked, and the magic leg had splintered and my father fell as if shot, and someone came off the bench and broke the German's jaw with a punch, and then they were pulling slats off the wooden fence

to tie against the ruined leg and waiting for an hour and a
half for the ambulance to come from Kings County Hospital
while they played out the rest of the game. The players and
the spectators were poor; not one of them owned a car. And
then at the hospital, he was dropped in a bed, twenty-eight
years old and far from home, and there were no doctors
because it was the weekend. Across the room, detectives
were questioning a black man whose stomach had been
razored open in a fight; and the ceiling reeled and turned,
his face felt swollen and choked, he remembered his father's
white beard and lifting bricks in the mason's yard; remembered all that, and the trip down the hill that day with the
clothes in the bag, dodging the British soldiers, heading for
a certain place where a certain man would get him on the
boat to Liverpool and then to America; remembered that,
he said later, and remembered how the razored man died in
silence, and there was no feeling in the magic leg. When the
doctors finally showed up the next morning, the leg was
bursting with gangrene, and they had to slice the soccer boot
off with a knife, and in the afternoon they took the leg off
above the knee. When he talked about it later, he never mentioned the pain. What he remembered most clearly was the
sound of the saw.

"Fried, Peter, or scrambled?"

I went into the kitchen. My mother was at the stove.
Denis stood in silence in a corner, staring at me. I went into
the L-shaped bathroom, with the swan decals on the walls,
and the pull-chain box up high near the ceiling. I closed the
door and felt tight and comfortable as I started to shave.
And I knew that he shaved there too, every morning, shaved,
and washed his face hard with very hot water so that his
skin was shiny and gleaming, and then combed his hair very
tightly, so that it was slick, black, glossy. And I wondered
if he ever stood there and thought about me.

I wondered whether he cursed the vanished leg, the terrible Sunday at Wanderers' Oval, and whether he was sorry because he never could do the things with me and Tommy that fathers were expected to do in America. He had never played baseball with us, or thrown us a pass with a football. We had never gone fishing, or wandered around Brooklyn on long walks, or gone on rides to the country, because he never learned to drive a car. He was a stranger to me, though we shaved at the same mirror, often with the same razor, and I had come to love him from a distance. I loved him when he would come home with his friends and sit in the kitchen drinking cardboard containers of beer, talking about fights, illustrating Willie Pep's jab on the light cord or throwing Ray Robinson's hooks into the wash on the kitchen line. I loved the hard defiance of the Irish songs, and I would lie awake in the next room listening to them, as they brought up the old tales of British malignance and murders commited by the Black and Tans and what the men in the trench coats did in the hours after midnight. But I didn't really know him, and I was certain he didn't know me. I had some bald facts: he had left school at twelve to work as a stonemason's apprentice, because there were eleven children in the family; he had been in Sinn Fein, and a policeman had been murdered, and he came on the run to America; for a while he struggled with night school at Brooklyn Tech, with my mother helping him with spelling. But I was seventeen and a half, and I still didn't know when they had been married, whether my mother was pregnant with me at the time, whether they had been married at all. There were no anniversary parties, and no wedding pictures on the walls. I tried not to care. But he didn't know really how to deal with me, didn't know what to do when I asked for help, and in many ways he was still Irish and I was an American. But I loved the way he talked and the way he stood on a corner with a

fedora and raincoat on Sunday mornings, the face shiny, the
hair slick under the hat, an Irish dude waiting for the bars
to open, and I loved the way he once hit a guy with a ball-bat
because he had insulted my mother. I just never knew if he
loved me back.

8.

I sat down to eat, and then heard him coming up
the stairs. He worked across the street in the Globe Lighting
Company, which took most of the third floor of the Ansonia
Clock Building, once the largest factory in Brooklyn, to us a
dirty red-brick pile. He was a wirer, a member of Local 3 of
the International Brotherhood of Electrical Workers; but
basically he was just another pair of hands on the assembly
line, and sometimes in the night he would come home, after
working all day on those concrete floors, and he would take
off the wooden leg, and the stump sock, and lie back on the
bed, the flesh of the stump raw and blistered; I never heard
him complain; he would just lie there, hurting, his hands
touching the bedsheets as if afraid to touch the ruin of the
leg, as if admitting pain would be some ultimate admission
that the leg was gone forever and he was mortal and growing old. Before the war he worked at the Roulston's plant,
down on Smith Street, a clerk, because the Irish came to
America with good handwriting, as they called it; he would
bring home mysterious bundles, sometimes wrapped in newspapers and tied with twine, containing canned food or
packaged spaghetti, and he would hand them to my mother,
always in silence, explaining nothing. He left Roulston's for
the war plant, and then there were a couple of years after

the war, made up of uncertainty, idleness, Rattigan's, the attempt to make something of the apartment on Seventh Avenue, where we had all moved in 1943; everything was always being painted, because the rumor was that fresh coats of paint would kill the eggs of the cockroaches; the kitchen table and the chairs were painted with Red Devil red, a coat a year, with newspapers spread out on the linoleum floors, and the walls were painted, and the closets; but the roaches still came, long and sleek and heavy with eggs, chocolate-brown, dark blond, plump and long and sometimes wedge-shaped, invincible, insidious, silent: and there is a dream I still have about a cockroach that moves into my ear at night, and gnaws its way to my brain, chewing, silent, its feelers humming and tentative, moving around in the crevices, an inhabitant of my skull.

"Hello, Magee."

He was in the door, with the familiar rolling limp, wearing a lumberjack's coat and a flannel shirt, hatless, the hair slicked back, and I got up and went over to him, and he shook my hand. My mother was behind us, making American cheese standwiches while tomato soup heated in a saucepan.

"Hey, you look good," he said, and he stepped back.

"They feed you pretty good there," I said.

"They must," he said. He had the jacket off now, and was sitting down, reaching for a steaming cup of tea. Denis put his head on my father's lap, and he rubbed the boy's head.

"You hear about O'Malley?"

"No, what?"

"The son of a bitch is taking the Dodgers out of Brooklyn."

"Billy," my mother said. "The language . . ."

"They're goin' to California," he said. "Him and the other son of a bitch, Stoneham. In a couple of years . . ."

"I don't believe it."

"Tommy Holmes had it in the *Eagle*."

"What for? I mean, why are they goin' out there?"

"Because O'Malley is a greedy son of a bitch, that's why."

My mother had sliced the sandwich in quarters and placed it before him, and he started to eat. Denis wandered into the other room.

"The players oughtta go on strike," he said. "Just say they're staying, and to hell with O'Malley. Never would've happened with Branch Rickey. He was a man, Rickey. Loved baseball, too. Put together the best bloody farm system in history."

"Yeah."

"Archie Moore's fighting Maxim this week, title fight."

"Moore should flatten him."

"I don't know," he said. "Maxim's a clever guinea. And Jack Kearns doesn't take any chances. Some manager, that Kearns. He managed Dempsey, you know. And Mickey Walker."

"But he can't break an egg with a punch, Maxim."

"He holds, and grabs ya, and it's hard to bang him. It's no cinch for Moore. He hasn't made the weight in two years."

"What did you think of the election?"

"I didn't like Stevenson."

"You mean you voted for a Republican?"

"Ike was a hell of a general," he said flatly. "Even if he looks like someone's aunt."

"He sounded pretty dumb, compared to Stevenson."

"He was a hell of a general," he said. There was a note

of finality in the statement; I remember it as a moment when I realized he was changing, because there wasn't a general who ever lived that Billy Hamill could admire. He was an enlisted man for life. I picked up the light zipper jacket.

"Well, I'll see you later," I said.

"Right," he said, without looking up.

I went out, moving quickly down the stairs, trembling.

9. It was a winter Saturday, heavy and sullen, with a wind blowing from the harbor. It felt like snow. I stepped out and turned right, heading for Sanew's Candy Store, to make the phone call. I hated the telephone, hated the whole mechanical ritual: the dime, the dialing, the distended, bodiless voice, the lack of smell and touch and sight. But this phone call was worse than the others.

The afternoon papers were already up, the *Post*, the *Journal-American*, and the *World-Telegram*, but I didn't see the *Compass*. That was the paper I read before I went away, along with the *Post*. They didn't sell many copies of either paper in that neighborhood; some of them felt that Joe Stalin was the editor of the *Post* and that the *Compass* was flown in every morning from the Kremlin. Others thought that the *Tablet* was the ideal middle-of-the-road newspaper (although my friends all used it as a shopping guide for movies marked "condemned"). I liked the *Post* because it had Jimmy Cannon and Herblock, and the *Compass* because it had run Bill Mauldin's drawings from Korea; one of the first books I stole from the library was

Mauldin's *Up Front* with its beautiful drawings of foot soldiers and incompetent generals. From the cartoons and the
comic strips I worked my way into the rest of the paper, to
I. F. Stone and some other wild men. They were always
talking about Whittaker Chambers and the Korean War,
Alger Hiss, and price controls and Richard Nixon; there
were people in the world named John Foster Dulles, people
who were described by my father's friends as "guys who
part their names in the middle," and they would certainly
do you no good. Eisenhower was about to become President,
the Democrats were in disgrace, and none of it made very
much sense to me, although I loved the argument and the
passion. The *Compass* had been the *Star*, and the *Star* had
grown out of the wreckage of *PM*, and standing at the news-
stand, I missed all of them. Mrs. Sanew, a thin, contained
Lithuanian woman, stared out at me as if I were about to
steal every paper there. I started to go in when I heard
somebody calling my name.

It was Brian and Johnny, racing from the corner, both
of them wearing mackinaws. They came on a run, and
leaped at me, and I hugged them and lifted them.

"Hey, where's your uniform?" Brian said.

"Upstairs in the closet."

"Aw, why didn't you wear it?"

"Didn't feel like it. Come on. Let's get an egg cream."

We went into the store. Mrs. Sanew stood aside, wary
and noncommittal. The kids jumped up on the stools. The
comic-book rack was to the left, and the telephone booth
was in the back.

"Four egg creams," I said. "The best you can make."

"I want Kits," John said.

"Naah, not Kits," I said. "You'll ruin your teeth. What
about a pretzel?"

"Yeah, yeah, pretzels."

I took three pretzels out of the can and laid them on the marble counter, while Mrs. Sanew made the egg creams. She stirred them with a long spoon and then placed them in front of the kids. I was still standing. She left her hand on the counter, waiting for the money. I handed her a dollar bill, and waited for change.

"You home for Christmas or for good, Peter?" Brian said.

"Not for good. Just for Christmas."

"Awww. Don't go back there, Peter."

"I have to, Brian."

Mrs. Sanew dropped the change. I picked up a dime.

"All right, no fooling around, you guys. I gotta make a phone call."

I went to the phone, waited, then dropped the coin in and dialed. It rang three times. I was about to hang up when her mother answered.

"Hello?"

"Oh, hello, Mrs. Crowley. It's Pete."

"Pete?"

"Pete—you know, Kathleen's boyfriend. Is she there?"

"Oh. Pete. Oh, *Pete!* Well, how are you, Pete?"

"I'm fine, Mrs. Crowley. Is—"

"How is the Navy treatin' you?"

"It's all right, Mrs. Crowley. Is . . . Kathleen there?"

"She's at school."

"On Saturday?" I didn't believe her.

"Oh, it's somethin' special, class day, or exams, or something like that."

"I see. Well, I guess I'll go down there and see her after school . . ."

"Pete?"

"Yes?"

"Did you get our Kathleen's letter?"

"Uh, yes, I did, Mrs. Crowley. Uh, which *one?*"

I knew exactly which one she meant.

"Well, the *last* one, son."

"Yes, I did. But, well, I still want to see her, Mrs. Crowley. I mean, that was while I was *away* and now I'm home and—"

"Well, I don't want you to get hurt, son."

"Yes. Yes, I know what you mean, Mrs. Crowley. Well, thanks. Nice talking to you."

I hung up and stood for a long moment in the phone booth. *I don't want you to get hurt, son.* Something moved and flopped over in my stomach, and I thought of how Kathleen's letters had come every day at the beginning, and then every other day, until they tailed off, and how their tone was warm and then ambiguous and then dutiful; they were like the letters I got from my mother when I was eleven and in the PAL camp in the Adirondacks. *We lived in Madrid Street and my father had red hair.* I put a finger into the coin-return slot. It was empty.

10. Brian was off the stool now.

"Hey, Peter, we gonna get a Christmas tree this year?"

"Absolutely."

"Let's get it today."

"Nah, I gotta go somewhere."

"They got them for two dollars over on Ninth Street."

"Maybe we'll go tomorrow."

I picked up the rest of the change; in that neighborhood, you never tipped.

"Hey, there's Daddy," Johnny said.

He was walking slowly across the street, heading back to the factory, the ruined leg stiff and dragging behind him. He had his head down, his hands jammed into the pockets of the lumber jacket. He looked very alone.

11. I took the bus down to St. Joseph's, sitting at a window seat in the back, watching the neighborhood slide by. The bus passed the Methodist Hospital, where my brothers had been born, and I wondered about the obscure, mysterious place where I had been born: never mentioned, never spoken of in detail—just a date, and some murky talk about Bay Ridge and a church called Our Lady of Perpetual Help where I had been baptized. I remember a cold wind blowing through me on the bus, and the familiar buildings, the grocery stores, luncheonettes and candy stores all rolling by without precision, and the cold wind blowing around the bus, chilling me. I tried to warm myself by thinking of Kathleen. All I felt was the presence of that wind.

The bus turned into Flatbush Avenue, and the long broad avenue stretched before us, sloping to the sea, and the Manhattan Bridge, and the spires of the city beyond. That was New York. When we talked about going to Manhattan we talked about going "over New York." It was some ancient way of speaking, from the days when Brooklyn was a separate city, rising on the hills facing the bay, a burgher city, with church spires and low buildings and more sky than any place around it. But the city had annexed Brooklyn before I was born, and it reeled away and never recovered,

and now, riding forward, the bus wheezing, the other passengers bundled up, the cold wind blowing, there was talk
that the Dodgers were leaving, that Furillo and Snider and
Cox and the rest of them were leaving town, heading for the
Coast, for California, for the Pacific and the sun.

And I knew the desire, because I had constructed so
many visions of the sun: Mexico and South America, dark
Spanish women, guitar nights, palm fronds blowing in the
tropic breeze; all of it made up out of books, and movies
with Jon Hall, long Saturday afternoons in the dark of the
Minerva and the Sanders and the Prospect. In those movie
houses, wonder awaited me; and as the bus moved past the
Carlton movie house, the Atlantic, the Terminal, as we came
into the business district where the Brooklyn Paramount
was, along with the RKO Albee, Loew's Met, the Duffield,
the Fabian Fox, a garish montage spilled through my mind,
fragments, jewels, pieces of *Gunga Din* and *King Kong*,
great glittering islands, Dr. Cyclops, the water hole in *Four
Feathers*, the charge of the Fuzzy Wuzzies, and Audrey
Hepburn: thin and elegant on her Roman Holiday, and Gene
Kelly playing an Irish-American painter in Paris, in love
with a ballerina, and dancing on the stone stairs beside the
Seine. In the dark, they touched me. In the dark, Audrey
Hepburn held me to her, her thin arms and long swan's neck
pressed against me, saying my name in a soft and tender
voice, and she was in my own small bed in an apartment in
Rome, with the sounds of music coming up from the street,
always kind, with intelligent eyes; Audrey Hepburn, sitting
in a maroon coat on a park bench in Prospect Park, as the
path curved away to Monument Hill, saying to me, in the
tender voice: Rome. Rangoon. Madrid. Milan. Paris. Bali.
Algeciras. All the strange names of the places of the earth,
all the places of cobalt-blue oceans and bruise-colored skies,

all the places where you smelled cocoa on the wind and no
footprints scarred the sand, where language was smooth as
a woman's slip, and nobody said your name except the
woman who was with you, long, thin, elegant and gentle,
Audrey Hepburn, holding my hand and saying my name.

The bus stopped in front of Abraham and Straus and
almost everybody got off, including me. And then we were
swamped by Christmas. All the department stores were
covered with lights and glitter, great golden wreaths, moun-
tains of pine twisted into tree shapes, Santa Claus and elves
and fairy princesses dancing in the windows. There were
clothes, electric trains, piles of toys, and mothers hustling
along with children behind them, moving into the stores,
bringing the children to see Santa. I moved past it quickly,
crossing Fulton Street against the light, dodging cars, and
turning into the street where Kathleen's school was. Suppose her mother had been lying? I imagined her sitting at
another chair in the kitchen while her mother lied. Or perhaps school was already out, it was a half-day, she was
already gone, and she would never answer the telephone
again, and I would spend this weekend without her. I wondered if she would talk to me, or whether she would brush
me off and walk into the crowds with her friends. I would
stand there, humiliated, in a crowd of girls, with the mean
stern faces of the nuns staring in approval from the
windows.

At the corner I stopped. The school was halfway down
the block, and a few girls had just walked out. Then another
bunch came out and then a flood. For a long moment I
wanted to go back, to disappear into the crowds of the
shopping district, or hide in the darkness of Loew's Met.

Then I saw her. She was wearing the maroon coat, and
talking to friends, and coming out of the main door, at the

top of a high stoop. Above the door, chiseled into stone, were
the initials IHS. I started across the street, moving through
the girls. Some seemed very young, freshmen, small girls
with braces and freckled faces and nervous sexless laughter;
there were older kids with acne and a touch of lipstick, and
then the seniors, some with dark experienced faces, others
already assuming the poses of wives and mothers. Kathleen
was at the bottom of the steps now, standing there, talking,
books cradled in her arms. She turned and saw me.

"Hiya," I said, and stepped forward. I'll never forget
her face. I don't remember what she said, but I remember
the face: shock, guilt, pity, all running under the delicate
features like underground rivers, followed by a tense strug-
gle for control, an attempt to freeze her face into an attitude
she could handle. Her friends stepped back, their faces like
the faces of people who had just witnessed an accident, with
the added quality that they knew it was coming, that they
had shared the fear of this moment with Kathleen, their
friend, and now wanted to protect her and couldn't move. I
tried to touch her hand. She stepped back, not looking at me,
staring at the ground, until I felt that somehow I had done
something terrible to her, that whatever this all meant, the
fault was mine.

"Let's go home," I said, looking at her friends as if
asking permission. But she turned from all of us, and started
walking quickly in the other direction, and then started running in a thin, side-by-side loping style. Her hair flopped,
the way it did the night at the V.F.W. party.

And I went after her, pushing through the startled
crowd of girls, leaving them behind, trying to catch up to
her. She turned the corner. I turned after her, and couldn't
see her. I went down the block. She was standing in a door-
way, leaning against the window of a shuttered electrical
supply store, her head lolling on her neck, her long body

limp, crying hard and long and hopelessly. I took her books
out of her hand and put my arm around her. We started to
walk, her head tight against my chest. Gray clouds moved
across the sky. It felt like snow.

12.
I don't remember precisely what it was I said
to her or what she said to me, but I remember a swirl of
buildings, and the two of us moving through the old meat-
market area behind the Long Island Rail Road, walking up
the long hill, trying to kiss her, and the way she turned her
head away. I remember that: and walking into Prospect
Park at Grand Army Plaza, the pathways empty and for-
lorn, and Kathleen trying to talk, and then stopping herself,
and then trying again. She loved to read my letters, she said,
with all the funny things and the descriptions of the sailors
and the drawings up and down the side. Yes: she loved those
letters, and she was sorry she didn't write every day, but
there were so many things on her mind, and how was my
mother, and where was my brother going to high school, and
did I think I would be going to Korea?

We plunged deep into the park, moving over hills, and
I knew that it was over. She talked about how I was in the
Navy and she was still in high school, and it was better this
way. I said what way? And she said this way, being friends,
maybe seeing each other when I was home. But I don't want
it that way, I said. Don't you see I love you? It eddied back
and forth like that, her weakness and vulnerability and con-
fusion, and then mine; me comforting her, she comforting
me. And I tried to tell her that I was going to be an artist, a
painter maybe, and we could live in Paris, which I had been

reading about in the library at Bainbridge. I talked about
these two writers, Hemingway and Fitzgerald, and some
woman writer named Gertrude Stein, and I mentioned a
book called *Left Bank, Right Bank,* by Joseph Barry, which
made it all seem as if the capital of the world were on the
Left Bank of the Seine. But we're only seventeen, she said.
That doesn't matter, I said. We can plan, we can make a life.
We can, I said, we really can. I read a book called *The Paris
Herald,* I said, about an American newspaper in Paris, and
maybe I could get a job there drawing cartoons and study
painting at the Sorbonne. When I got out of the Navy I
would have the GI Bill, and they pay you for going to school.
We could go there together and get a small apartment and
learn French and I could get an easel and set up right there
in the street, the way they did it in the pictures and the
movies. I want you to come with me, to wait for me until I'm
finished, and then come with me to Paris. Oh, Pete, we're
only seventeen. Couldn't we wait until you get discharged,
and then we could talk about it? But I didn't want to wait,
I told her, that would mean three and a half years, and I
wanted her to say yes now, and maybe we could even
get married. Just like Mickey Horan and Jackie McAlevy,
they were married, they were in the Navy and they were
married. Oh, Pete, she said, sad, her body bunching
up, as we came around the hill overlooking the big lake.
Oh, Pete.

   We sat on a bench in the cold, looking out over the lake,
the whole area deserted and gray, the heights of Monument
Hill rising behind us, while thin shelves of ice gathered at
the edges of the lake, like steam on a window.

   Was there another guy? I asked. And she sat there
quietly while I shivered in the light zipper jacket, and she
told me how it would be a good idea to finish high school in

the Navy and how her sister was sick with tuberculosis and
her father was opening another saloon down on Flatbush
Avenue. She never answered the question, and then, very
lightly, it started to snow.

"I've got to go home," she said.

"Please don't," I said. "Not now, not yet. Let's watch
the snow."

"I can't."

She got up. And I wanted her to wait there, to hold my
hands and my body, to stand there with me, while the snow
came piling down from the sky, a million wet flakes a minute, covering the meadows, drifting against the trees, a
great silent drowning of the city, piling around us, deeper,
wilder, all swirls and silence, with the two of us running in
it finally, across the broad covered meadows, packed with
warmth, snowshoes, gloves, impervious to the cold, en-
veloped by the blinding whiteness. She turned, alone, and
started to walk to the exit beside the playground, leading to
the last small block before home.

"Kathleen," I called after her.

I thought she would just keep going, without ever looking back. She waited.

"Kathleen, please—"

"You'll never understand," she said.

She glanced around, at the snow falling in the park, at
the entrance to Seeley Street, where she lived, at the Parkview Bar across the street.

"Just try to explain," I said.

"I can't. Oh, God, I can't."

And then she was gone. I watched her walk across the
street, into the tumbling whiteness, until I couldn't see her
any more, and I stood there for a long time, cold and desolate
and destroyed.

13.

I crossed the street and went into the Parkview and started to drink. The Parkview was one of the bars that served young people, and weren't too fussy about draft cards. On this Saturday afternoon, I didn't see any of my friends. I put a five on the bar and listened to a crowd of bricklayers arguing fights. Somebody made Moore a lock over Maxim, and somebody else said that this kid Floyd Patterson would beat the both of them, and then two iron-workers started to argue over the best way to operate a crane, and I started to feel drunk. Along the far wall were booths, and I had sat in one of them with Kathleen one sad night in the weeks before I left for the Navy. Someone shouted that the only good Communist was a dead Commu-nist, and everybody knew that Roosevelt was a Commie, a card-carrying Commie who let the Jews and the Commies take over the government for him. The Communists were all Jews, and the biggest mistake after the war was that Patton didn't keep on going, right into Russia, and destroy those bastards while they were still weak. He could've done it too, if it wasn't for the deal Roosevelt made with the Russians. I listened to all of this, at a spot near the door, while Bing Crosby crooned from the jukebox, singing "Tooralooraloora." And all the while the snow kept falling, coming down from the darkness now, a glistening shower as it passed the street lamps, coating the park. Once, I went to the men's room, and washed my hands when I was finished. I stared at my face in the mirror for a long time, wondering what it was, what she saw in that face that I didn't see, what it was that scared her or offended her, what it was that she no longer valued. And I started to cry, big heaving, wracking sobs, and just as quickly choked it off, drying my face with paper towels, afraid that someone would walk in and find me crying. And then I went back again to the bar, to the com-pany of men, where they were talking about Joe McCarthy and how Cushing said that if it looks like a duck and walks like a duck and talks like a duck, it must be a duck, and the same thing goes for the Communists. I stared out at the trees of the park, stark and skeletal against the snow, and wished I could draw them like that, etching them black against a hard brilliant white, and then I thought again of Paris.

I went to the phone booth at the back of the bar and called Kathleen. I told her that I loved her and I wouldn't go back to the Navy if that was what she wanted. I would go A.W.O.L, and we could move away, maybe out West somewhere, Arizona, or California, I could change my name, I could do that, and it would be all right, it really would, I would do all that, and we could be married and go away, honest to God. She hung up on me. I went back to the bar, picked up my change, and walked out into the snowy night.

14. I wanted to see my brother Tom, to talk to him, to see how he was, and what he was doing. But I didn't want to go home. Not then. Not after that. Tom and I, along with my sister, were part of the prewar family; the young kids were all born after the war. We had grown up close, until the year before, when I was able to go to the bars and he was still too young and too small to sneak in. But I wanted to tell him where I had been, and what it was like, things I couldn't put in letters and couldn't draw in pictures. Most of all I just wanted to see him; somehow I sensed that there might be other bad times on telephones and I might lose this slender girl, but my brother Tommy would still be there. I just didn't want to go home, didn't want to sit at the kitchen

table, and tell stories and listen to the children; didn't want
to risk my father's silence. But we had no telephone, so
Tommy would have to wait until morning.

I walked up the hill through the snow, running a finger
through the packed snow on the hoods of automobiles. On
this side of the hill, the houses were newer than on my side
of the hill; there were no tenements, no fire escapes scarring
the fronts of the buildings, and everybody had a backyard.
There were Christmas wreaths in the windows, and lights
running around the doors, blinking off and on, and in a
couple of houses the shades were up and I could see huge
Christmas trees, reaching to the ceilings, dazzling and gorgeous. I hated them. They lived in safety, defended against
the world; there were locks on their doors, and the men
went to work with suits on, and all their sons finished high
school and some even went to college. I would see them all
the time in the years when I was an altar boy at Holy Name,
full of piety, bribing their way into Heaven with donations
and purchased pews, with garlands of flowers on large occa-
sions and weekly ass-kissing with the priests. They had big
weddings for their daughters, and arrived with striped
pants and cutaway coats, and stood in the sacristy like
actors in a show. I remember feeling that if they were Cath-
olics, I didn't want to be one.

At the corner of Tenth Avenue, a small dark girl with
long glossy black hair came out of the snow. She was walking with her head down against the driving storm. Her name
was Betty Haddad, and she was a friend of Kathleen's. I
touched her hand, and she jumped nervously, then recog-
nized me.

"Oh, my God! *Pete*, how *are* you?"

"Great, great."

"I mean, when did you get home?"

"Last night, early this morning, real late."

"You look great." The snow was piling on her hair.

"You want to have a drink?" I said.

"A drink?"

"Yeah, I'm going over Boop's."

"I better not."

"Okay."

I started to go. She looked up at me.

"Did you see Kathleen?"

"Yeah. Yeah, I did. I went down to school and met her there." I shrugged. She knew what was going on.

"She's just mixed up is all, Pete."

"Me too." I shivered in the wind.

"Listen," she said, "I'm having a party Sunday night, tomorrow night. Why don't you come?"

"Is she going to be there?"

"I don't know. Maybe. I invited her."

"With somebody?"

"I don't think so."

"Ah, I better not."

"Suit yourself. But you're welcome, Pete."

"Thanks, Betty."

She was a bright, smiling girl, and I liked her a lot. I liked her more that night.

"I mean it," I said. "Thanks."

She moved into the storm.

15. Boop's was on the corner of Tenth Avenue and Seventeenth Street, a tight, packed noisy place filled with bookmakers and Italian hard guys. They had accepted us in the year before I went away, because we knew a lot about

fighters, and they lived for the fights on television. They didn't care that some of us were underage, as long as we carried the phony draft cards, and there was a back room with a few dusty booths where we could sit with our girls, play the jukebox, and even dance. The Four Aces were usually on the jukebox, with "Garden in the Rain" and "Tell Me Why" and "I Understand," but when I walked in, a group was singing a song called "Maybe."

> *"Maybe the one*
> *Who is waiting for you*
> *Will prove untrue.*
> *Then what will you do?"*

Boop was behind the bar, a large beefy man with streaks of gray in his hair, and he smiled when he saw me.

" 'Ey, Peter. 'Ey, welcome home." He started pulling a beer, and turned to some of the older guys at the end of the bar. " 'Ey, look who's home." The older guys all looked up, and shouted down the bar—welcome home, and good to see you, and how ya been—and Boop slid the beer in front of me and didn't take any change out of the dollar.

"The guys been around?" I said.

"Not yet. They'll be up later, I guess. We got the fight tonight, from Syracuse or some place. Miceli's goin' against some dinge."

"That's pretty good."

"He's got some left hook, that Miceli."

"A good banger," I said. "He oughtta leave the right hand in the dressing room but."

"I think he's got a weak left tit."

"That's what they say."

"Them good-looking guys, you know how it is. Either they're all fucked out, or they're thinkin' about it, or they don't wanna get their faces mussed. That Vince Martinez, the same thing."

"Him and Miceli is a good fight."

"They'd probably make a deal not to hit each other in the labonza unless it was absolutely necessary."

"Them mustache guys are all the same."

"No left tit, them guys," Boop said.

A couple of the older guys came in from the back room, and Boop turned to serve them. One of them was Porky, a tall, good-looking guy with straight black hair, who was about thirty. I always liked him, but the word around the neighborhood was that he had some funny friends. This wasn't unusual, of course, but I never asked about it; when we talked, it was about fighters, ball games, women, and drinking; I never asked him what he did for a living.

"Hey, Peter," he said, "how *are* ya?" He motioned to Boop to send me a refill. "Good luck, kid."

I raised the glass. "Cheers."

"Who do you like in the fight?"

"I don't even know who Miceli's fightin'."

"Bratton."

"Oh, wow. That's not good for Miceli."

"I hear Bratton's a shell," Porky said.

"He better be, for Joe's sake."

"We'll see. Talk to you later, kid. I got some guys with me."

> *Maybe.*
> *You'll sit and sigh,*
> *Wishing that I*
> *Were near. And then,*
> *Maybe you'll ask me,*
> *To come back again,*
> *And maybe I'll say,*
> *Maybe.*

I went to the phone and called Tim Lee, but he wasn't home. So I drank at the bar, staring at my face in the mirror, young behind the whiskey bottles. I wondered where my father was, whether he was at Rattigan's, and whether this was the night when I should go down there, for the first time, moving into his world as a man. The place was closed to us, one of those bars where the rules were strict, and one of the rules was that they wouldn't serve underage kids. It was more a club than a bar, and membership was easy to obtain, and it was a lot easier to lose. You didn't stiff bartenders, you didn't fool around with anyone's women, you always made sure a drunk got home safe, and you didn't hit a guy in the place unless he took a shot at you first. I knew the rules, all right; Boop's had rules like that, too, but it was an Italian joint and they were looser about a lot of things than the Irish. "I figure a guy's old enough to go in the Army," Boop said one night, "he's old enough to drink in my bar." But the cops never came near the place anyway; the bookmakers made sure of that.

> *I understand.*
> *And darling, you are not to blame.*
> *If when we kiss*
> *It's not the same.*
> *I understand.*

I tried to remember the first time I saw her, to understand why I was in love with her. It wasn't clear, and it was only a year before. I remembered other things: the beach at Oceantide, with the pitchers of beer on the tables, all of us eating sandwiches at Mary's, and the first moves into McLain's and McCabe's, the big Irish summer joints down the street. And she was with me: waiting on the line for the

sandwiches, dancing stiffly in the little fenced pen beside the
pool at Oceantide, the ride home on the trolley later; nights
in luncheonettes, drinking Cokes, or sitting on the benches
along the parkside, talking, or in silence.

"Kathleen . . ." I said it out loud, very quietly, but nobody heard; the boss and underboss players were working
hard around the corner table, and Porky and his friends
were deep in conversation. It was still snowing. I drained
the beer, and Boop filled it again.

"How's your girl, Pete? The thin one? What's her name
again?"

"Kathleen."

"That's right. You seen her yet?"

"Yeah. Today."

"She must be happy, huh?"

"I don't know, Boop."

He saw it on my face. "Uh-oh."

"It's all right," I said.

"Bullshit. It's never all right."

I leaned forward on the bar. "You're right, I guess."

"What happened? One of them Dear John Letters?"

"That's right."

"Well, that really pisses me off. A guy goes in the service, the least his broad could do is wait around. But they're
all wacky, you ask me. You get a nice broad, she acts like a
saint, she won't let ya touch her, not even feel her up, the
next thing ya know she's runnin' off with a guy in a raccoon
coat. They're all hoowiz, ya ask me. Don't let it get you down,
Pete. 'Ey, how about something to eat?"

"She's not a whore, Boop."

"Yeah, *I* know. *I* know what ya mean. Just don't let it
get you down, is all."

"I won't."

"You're a young guy. These things happen."

"Maybe I'll have a hot dog."

"How about two?"

He was cooking the hot dogs on an electric grill when the guys came in. All of them. Tim Lee, Boopie Conroy, Jimmy Doyle, Bobby Malloy. The Gremlins: Eddie Norris, Joe Griffin, four or five other guys. The place exploded with noise. The boss and underboss players started talking louder, and Porky and his friends went into the back room for a little quiet. I was glad to see everybody and they were glad to see me, and we started a dollar pool on the bar and started ordering ten beers at a time. Words spilled as quickly as the beer—camps, outfits, place names, Fort Benning and Fort Sam Houston, Pensacola, Norfolk, and places with stranger names: Seoul, the Chosin Reservoir, and over and over, Korea, out in that Korea, going to Korea. "Jesus Christ, I heard Buddy Kiernan got it over there, son of a bitch. I just seen him a couple a months ago. Got it just like that." "It's them bugles that scare me; I'd like to fight them man-to-man, out in the open, a fair one, but them bugles and them human waves, that's pretty scary, man." "What are we doin' there, anyway?" There were waterfalls of beer now, and I felt warm and cozy and protected. The fight went on, and it was over fast. Tim Lee, who worked in the gym every day, and was thinking of going in the Gloves, said you could've gotten wet if you sat at ringside: "That was the biggest splash in a tank since Willie lost to Lulu Perez." But someone said that Bratton was over as a fighter, used up, drinking and staying out of the gym, and someone else said that Miceli was a one-armed fighter and if he got too fresh, he better watch out, because Basilio was waiting. The night moved; the snow kept falling and steam was gathering in the front windows of the bar. Once I dialed the first four letters of

Kathleen's number and then changed my mind and had
another hot dog instead; the hot dogs were baked and dry,
not like the great juicy dogs of Nathan's, and someone said
they were sending out for a pizza, a quarter a piece, and
then the pizza arrived, and then I found myself sitting on a
stool, the bar moving and rolling around me, as I played
with my change, making circles on the top of the wet bar,
placing the dimes and quarters in geometric arrangements,
and realizing suddenly that even there, surrounded by my
friends, I was still alone. I could never admit to them that I
had cried that afternoon over a woman, could never explain
the dreams of Paris, the garret on the Left Bank, the
dreams of foreign places, the long romantic afternoon I had
planned for my life, and the hole in it that Kathleen left.
They were realistic men, and they would have laughed at me.
They knew that in that neighborhood, you became a cop
or a fireman or an ironworker, or maybe you ended up in the
can; you dreamed no large dreams.

> *I understand*
> *And darling, you are not to blame,*
> *If when we kiss, it's not the same . . .*

I couldn't explain how songs worked themselves into
me, or about the strange new books I had been reading while
I was away, about Gatsby and Lady Brett and Catherine
Barkley; or about my mother sitting alone at the kitchen
table in the deep of night, or the strange hard separation
between me and my father.

"Hey, Peter, babe, I hear Kathleen is goin' with Tommy
Riggs these days!" It was Joe Griffin, a short, laughing guy
who looked like Red Buttons, and lived down Prospect Avenue near Seeley Street.

"Oh, yeah?" I said. "Where'd you hear that?"

"I don't know, around, you know."

"I didn't hear that."

"Oh, hey, I'm sorry."

"Forget about it, Joe."

"You didn't know, really?"

"No."

"I mean, she didn't *tell* you?"

"No."

"No shit?"

"No shit."

Boop brought us some beers; the bar was moving and turning now, and I was afraid to get up; thinking of Tommy Riggs, tall, with squinty eyes, broad-shouldered, good with his hands.

"Ah, the hell with it, Pete. Ass is ass. They're all the same under the covers."

"Where's Riggs?"

"He's on a can in Norfolk."

"You know if he's home this weekend?"

"Hell, I don't know. But wait a minute, Pete . . ."

"You know where he lives?"

"Down the hill someplace, but listen, Pete, forget it. Whatta you want with that kind of trouble? I mean, what's it get you?"

"Satisfaction," I said.

After a while I went into the back room to see Porky. He was sitting in a booth with two of his friends, who were wearing gingerella hats and leaning forward, whispering. I asked if I could talk to him alone.

"Sure, kid," he said, getting up. We stood in the passageway between the crowded noisy bar and the empty back room.

"What's the problem?"

"I want a gun."

"No, you don't."

"I do."

"What for?"

"I want to kill a guy."

"Come on, kid. That's pretty silly."

"I have to kill this guy, Porky."

"Why?"

"He moved in on my girl."

"That's about the worst reason I ever heard for wantin' ta kill a guy."

"I got to."

"Kid, listen ta me. You're what? Seventeen, eighteen? You're what? In the Navy? Take my advice. See the world. Get laid. Forget this bitch, whoever she is."

He patted me on the shoulder and went back to his friends. I went back to mine. We closed Boop's that night, and Timmy Lee and Joe Kelly and I left together, to go back to the Seventh Avenue end of the neighborhood, marching through the piled snow, falling and sliding and drunk. I woke up in the morning on the couch with a thick tongue and dirty fingernails, my shoes clouded and wet from the snow, and I couldn't remember coming home. There was someone I was supposed to call, but I couldn't remember who it was. It certainly wasn't my lost girl.

16. My brother Tommy and I took a walk around the neighborhood at noon. He was going to Brooklyn Tech and wanted to be a scientist, and I loved his cool intelligence. He was much smaller than me physically, which made it hard for him to begin the ritual of admission to the bars, so he forced his energy into his work. We wandered up past the factory, along Twelfth Street to the park, and I told him about the books I was reading and how he ought to pick up on them, and he told me about the teachers he had at Tech, how much better they were than the Xaverian brothers we had in Holy Name. I remembered one time when we were younger, and we played blind man's bluff on Eleventh Street, and Tommy had the blindfold tied around his head, very small, very vulnerable, and how he had walked out into the street, and a car had screeched away from him; I felt responsible, as if I had set him up to be killed, and I would dream about that summer afternoon all my life.

We ended up at Lewnes', a large soda fountain and restaurant on Bartel-Pritchard Square, where the crowd always went after Mass. Or rather the girls went after Mass, because most of the guys didn't bother any more. I hadn't been at Mass since I was fifteen, and Tommy stopped going when he was thirteen. We told my mother we had gone, if she asked, but it wasn't any big deal. I just didn't like the people: the pompous, bullying priests, and the slick pampered men from the houses on the other side of the hill, and I didn't believe it was right to have gold chalices on an altar when people on Seventh Avenue didn't even have backyards.

Tommy and I stood in front of Lewnes' for a while, in an area scraped clean of snow. The park looked gorgeous: white as far as you could see, with children already sliding down the hills on sleds, and great armies of them pouring from all of the streets leading to the park.

"Mom's got problems," Tommy said.

"I know."

"She doesn't have any money, Pete. Not a dime."

"Whatta you mean? Dad's workin' overtime."

"He lost some days, and I don't know, she just doesn't have enough."

"You mean for Christmas?"

"Yeah." He was watching the middle-class kids arrive at the entrance to the park, walking quietly between the two large Roman columns we called the totem poles. "I got an answer."

"You do?" I said.

"Maybe we could borrow a gun."

He wants a gun too. "And what would we do with a gun?"

"Stick up a place."

"Me and you?"

"Why not?"

I remembered the talk with Porky, knowing that if I had been handed a gun the night before, I would have used it.

"Forget it," I said. "We'd be the first ones caught."

"Well, what else are we gonna do?"

"I don't know. Let me think about it. But guns ain't the solution, that's for sure."

The first guys started coming around, Duke Baluta, Conroy, Billy Powers, home on leave from the Air Force. Some of them were a few years older than I was, and the spread between them and Tommy seemed enormous.

"I feel like I spent the night lickin' a pool table," Conroy said. "What time did we get out of that place?"

"I don't remember," I said.

"I read in the paper that's a sure sign of an alcoholic," Duke said. "You can't remember how you got home. They say it means that you damaged your brain tissues. I swear. It was in the papers. Would I shit you?"

"People who don't drink write that stuff," Conroy said. "Guys who have to drink in the morning, they're alcoholics."

"Nah," Duke said, "the worst people are the people who drink alone. Especially those winos. They sit in the kitchen, all alone, and they drink that muscatel. You ever taste that stuff? It's like pelican piss."

"What do you know about pelican piss, Duke?"

"Nothin'," he said. "But I can imagine."

"You see the fight?"

"Bratton should of had a life preserver, goin' in the tank that big."

"An Academy Award performance."

"I hear Paddy Young went swimmin' too," I said. "A couple of weeks ago."

"Yeah," Duke said. "It was in Dan Parker in the *Mirror*. He was goin' in the Army, so he grabbed a payday. He went out with a right to the elbow."

"Nobody was better than Willie Pep, with Lulu."

"They picked up his license but."

"It was pretty bad," I said.

"Even Lulu couldn't believe it," Conroy said.

A group of girls were coming across the circle, past the benches, all wearing long coats and boots. Kathleen wasn't with them.

"Wow, I would like this one to sit on my face," Duke said. "Just sit there."

He was looking at a plump, bright-eyed girl named Eileen. She had large breasts swelling under the coat, and good teeth. It didn't matter that she would grow up fat.

"Fifteen gets you thirty," someone said. Eileen was about sixteen.

"It would be worth it, believe me," Duke said.

She walked past us, shooting us a mildly salacious glance, and went into the ice-cream parlor.

"Marrone!"

"Whadda they feed these kids?"

"I'd eat her in a minute. She wouldn't even hafta wash."

"What lung warts."

It went on like that for a while, until we all decided to go in and have some coffee. Tommy had to go home. It wasn't his crowd.

"I'll be down the house," he said.

"You got school tomorrow?" I asked him.

"Nah, I'm off till after New Year's."

"Maybe we'll go down Pearl Street. Look at the books."

"I don't have any money, Pete."

"Let me see what I can do."

"We better give it to Mom."

"How much you think we need?"

"I don't know. Forty, fifty bucks."

"Let me think about it."

He left, walking along the parkside in the snow. I went into Lewnes' and walked to the back where the guys were sitting in a booth, kidding around with the Greek waiter about the girls on the other side of the center partition. It was warm in the place, and I took off my jacket. I wished I owned an overcoat.

17.
That night I went to the party at Betty Haddad's house. She lived in the top floor of a good prewar apartment house at the foot of Windsor Place, an apartment house with locked front doors and elevators and steam heat that had been there from the beginning. The house was nicely furnished, with a lot of wood, candlesticks and Persian rugs,

and our crowd couldn't get over the fact that there were two bathrooms. Betty's father was in the rug business, or something, the way most of the Syrian Christians seemed to be. Most of the people there called her an Arab, which she was, and she didn't have a steady guy.

I didn't own a suit, so I took the zipper jacket off when I came in, and started drinking Rheingold out of cans. It's difficult to explain just how cramped and uncomfortable those parties were; girls together, girls with their men away in the service, refusing even to dance with other guys, and the guys, after a while, not bothering to even ask them, and getting drunk instead. I remember the party vaguely at best: sitting on a couch, knocking ashes onto the Persian rugs, stabbing at the cheese like it was a sworn enemy, leaving cans on the bookcases, and dancing hard, wild, driving lindies—legs kicking out hard, throwing the women around like dolls. Betty Haddad danced the best, in what was called "Lyceum style," intricate, difficult, all hands and fast breaks, and we danced while the party filled up and the overhead lights went out, leaving a golden diffused look from the lamps and the wood, dancing furiously, sweat pouring off me, my shirt sticking to me, feeling the muscles bunching and expanding the way they did in a boxing ring: until I looked up and saw Kathleen, walking in the door with Riggs, not looking at me, smiling and nervous, while Riggs took her coat. I slowed the dance, and then stopped, and Betty knew what had happened. She held my hand tightly.

Riggs was wearing his Navy uniform, three white stripes on the sleeve indicating that he had been in at least a year longer than I. The uniform was tightly tailored, showing off the lean, hard body. Some of the girls looked up when they came in, and fell silent, but the music was driving over everything. I let go of Betty's hand and walked over.

"Hello, Kathleen," I said.

"Hi, Pete," she said, looking embarrassed and helpless. Riggs was staring at me, but I was looking at Kathleen.

"Do you want to dance?" I asked her. I felt crude and abrupt.

"I can't," she said. "I'm with Tommy."

"Okay," I said. I went back into the living room. I felt foolish, certain that everyone was watching me, the girls more than the others. The place filled up again with movement and dancing, and I stood next to the phonograph, drinking a can of beer, my back to Kathleen and Riggs. I noticed dirt under the nails on my right hand, and started cleaning them with a matchbook cover. I drained the beer and went into the kitchen for another. And coming from deep inside me, I felt something high and white, a high singing sound, in my ears, in the space between my brain and my skull, made up of loss, animal rage, anger, murder. It rose and ebbed, and then rose again, stronger, and I touched a sideboard and held on.

Duke came in. "You seen the churchkey?" he said. "I can't find a churchkey."

I had an unopened can in my hand. "I'm looking for it myself, Duke."

"Syrians don't drink," Duke said. "I swear ta God. They don't drink nothing. It's against their religion."

"Betty's a Catholic," I said. "She was in my class in Holy Name."

"I thought they were Arabs. You know, they sit around eating halvah."

I started to laugh, and the anger went out of me. We found a can opener in a drawer, opened the cans, and went back to the party. Kathleen was sitting next to Riggs on the couch at the other end of the room; I stood with Duke for a while, watching her in quick jerking glances through the pile of dancers. She seemed stiff and controlled. Riggs had a leg across his knee, a cigarette in his left hand, a whiskey in his right; he seemed to swagger as he sat there. In my head, I walked through the dancers, removed the cigarette, lifted the glass, and punched him savagely as he sat there, listening to him whine, feeling things break as I hit him. Betty came over again, and I drained my beer, and started to dance. She held me very close to her, and I put my head in her hair, smelling soap and perfume. It was darker in the room now, and the music was slow and lonely and lush with violins. It was Billy Eckstine.

> *The night is like a lovely tune*
> *Beware my foolish heart.*
> *How white, the ever-constant moon*
> *Beware my foolish heart.*

"Forget it," she said.
"I'm tryin'."

> *There's a line between love and fascination*
> *That's hard to see on an evening such as this*
> *For they both give the very same sensation*
> *When you're lost in the magic of a kiss . . .*

Her small hard breasts were against my chest, and I had my hand inside the back of her blouse, touching her skin. The room was spinning, all mauves and dark blues. Her skin was damp. I moved her around so that Kathleen could see us.

"Just for a while . . ."
"I can't."

For this time it isn't fascination . . .

The music wound down, Frank Sinatra came on singing
"Castle Rock," I opened another beer, we danced again.
Betty drifted around emptying ashtrays. Two girls got up,
and ran to the bathroom, one of them crying. Bobby Malloy
knocked a bowl of peanuts off a table, and someone ground
them into the rug. I was very hungry. In the kitchen, Jimmy
Doyle and Timmy Lee were arguing over the Moore-Maxim
fight. I moved along the wall, still not looking at Kathleen
and Riggs. Somehow, the kitchen became the focus of the
party, as the guys with girls stayed dancing, and the girls
with guys away in the service sat together on the chairs and
couches. Malloy started a two-dollar pool for more beer.
Cans covered all the surfaces: some half empty, others with
cigarette butts smashed at their lips, others filled with warm
beer. The fresh cases arrived, and I felt myself getting
drunk. Betty walked into the kitchen and I grabbed at her;
she bent away from me. All of it wordless. I started out
after her, and saw Kathleen. Riggs had his arm around her
and was kissing her. I went into the bedroom and searched
through the overcoats until I found the zipper jacket. I
bumped into the doorframe on the way out of the bedroom,
and had trouble with the lock on the front door, I felt myself
start to cry, but I fought it down and went out into the
snow.

18. And so for a week I retreated into the city, walking the streets, holing up in movie houses and bookstores. At night I would stop in Boop's for a few beers, but the workingmen weren't around and the guys were pairing off with girls, going with them to movies or to the department stores for Christmas shopping. I moved alone, luxuriating in it, freezing out what had happened. I wondered about Riggs and Kathleen. But when I started to think about it, I would pick up a book and read. Meanwhile, Christmas was moving closer. The snow had turned to a foul oatmeal-colored slush, but people still talked about a white Christmas.

I had twenty-two dollars left from the Christmas-leave money. One night I asked Tim Lee if he thought he could get me about forty dollars somewhere. It was a lot of money in that neighborhood; he said he would ask his brother Mike, who was an ironworker, and he would let me know. I really couldn't ask him for money and drink with him, so I would go off alone.

After a few days I started to think of myself as a secret agent, moving among people who saw my face but didn't know my true identity. My papers said Hamill, citizen of United States, member of United States Navy, seventeen, 167 pounds. But they were false. I came from Paris, the movies, the IRA; that was me moving in the darkness of Belfast, with the sten gun under the trench coat and the wool cap pulled down against the Irish rain; that was me on the waterfront in Singapore, with a Eurasian woman waiting in the opium house, while they loaded the spices and I waited for the rubies; I heard the waterfall in the distance, slow and rumbling, as we drifted down the Orinoco on a raft. *A jagged streak of lightning shot athwart the sky, followed by a deafening crash of thunder . . .*

I still thought about her, though, but only at night.

19. Three days before Christmas, Brian and Tommy and I went down to Fifth Avenue and bought the tree. It was puny by the standards of the other side of the hill, and we had to argue with the guys who were selling them off the back of stake trucks like hot suits. But it was a tree, and we carried it home through the wet streets, our hands gummy from the tar of the trunk.

My mother was out when we got there, but we started to set it up anyway. We didn't have money for lights, but we had a lot of angel hair and aluminum streamers and gaudy balls from other Christmases, and we garnished the tree, turning it into a small glittering object, and laid cotton on the floor underneath, and scotch-taped red-brick crepe paper to the fireplace. The smell of pine filled the room; Brian, John and Denis leaped about in excitement, moving the decorations and the balls from one branch to another, staring at their distorted reflections. We had an old wind-up Victrola and Tommy put on Bing Crosby's version of "Adeste Fideles" and it started to feel like Christmas.

"What do you want for Christmas, Denis?"

"Bandages!"

"What do you mean, bandages."

"He likes to wrap bandages around his head," Brian said.

"You mean adhesive-tape bandages?"

"Yeah, that stuff that sticks."

"What about you, John?"

"A train set."

"Brian?"

"A fielder's mitt."

"Wow, you guys want a lot of stuff."

"What about you, Pete?" Brian said.

I thought about it for a moment. "I don't know. I really don't know."

20.

My mother was pleased and saddened by the tree. It was there, and that pleased her, because it was fun for the kids. But it brought again the pressures of Christmas; she wanted so much to make those children happy that Christmas became the most difficult time of the year for her; she simply didn't have the money to buy anything fancy, no electric trains, fielder's mitts. She usually made do with stockings filled with tangerines and walnuts, bought on credit at Jack's grocery store, or managed to stretch her credit at one of the department stores. But every Christmas there seemed to be at least one more child to please, and it wasn't very easy. The women like her usually waited until Christmas Eve and headed for the stores on Fifth Avenue to get the remainders at cut rates, the way they showed up at Mrs. Wagner's for the broken pies or Larsen's Bakery for the day-old bread.

"God love you, it's beautiful," she said.

"It's a little skinny in the back."

"Sure, who would see that? It's lovely."

And she meant it; it was one of those moments when I wondered what she thought America was going to be like, back then, when she was growing up in Ireland, her mother widowed and then sick and then dead; living in Belfast as a Catholic, in the house on Madrid Street, thinking about going to the America where her father had died when she was six. I wondered if she knew then who she would marry and what her children would be like, where she would live and whether she would be rich or poor She arrived in America on the day the stock market crashed in 1929, and so most of her life the country had been a place of mean times. Somehow she endured; she started as an indentured servant, working off her passage as a servant to the rich. But she never spoke meanly about them. To her it was a fair deal. And she had the Church. It meant something to her, it was a living, breathing thing, and she went to Mass every Sunday, and did the Perpetual Novenas, and somehow even came up with a quarter for the weekly collections. But I had seen the way she lived, and the Church to me was a gigantic hoax, a collection of men who lived off the labor of the poor. When I was fifteen we argued about it, and then never mentioned it again.

"A really lovely tree," she said.

But my father said nothing. It was a tree to him. And he looked at it, and then went inside to sit down to dinner.

21. Two nights before Christmas, Tim Lee came around to call for me. I was out, sitting in the Prospect, smoking a cigar and watching Mario Lanza in *The Great Caruso*. The cigar was given to me by a fireman whose wife had just had a baby, and it was dry and flaky. The picture wasn't any good, but I liked the singing and when I came out into the brightness under the marquee, all the Italian guys were doing bits from *Pagliacci*. It was after midnight, and I started walking up Ninth Street to the park. For a moment I thought about going over to Rattigan's, to drink there for the first time. I kept walking up Ninth Street.

Lewnes' was deserted, so I walked up to Boop's. The streets were slick with ice. Farrell's was noisy and crowded as I went by, but that was another crowd. When I reached the top of the hill, I stood for a moment looking across the street at the church. It was a large red-brick building, with ivy climbing its sides, and a statue of Our Lady of Fatima in front. Around the corner there was an iron staircase lead-

ing to a side door that was used by the altar boys and the
funeral directors. A priest was at the side door now, locking
it, and I stopped and watched him for a moment. He was a
young priest, one I had never seen before. He came down
the stairs and saw me standing on the other side of the
mesh fence.

"Can I help you?" he said.

There was something soft and pampered about his face,
as if it were accustomed to good cologne.

"I don't think so."

No, I don't think so at all. You could go back up those
stairs and plunder the golden instruments; you could sell
away the fine brocaded vestments; you could come down off
the hill, down to where I live, and you could give money and
food to my people, in the name of your God. It wasn't my
God any more, but we would take whatever you had. Forty
dollars would be a good beginning.

"Is something the matter?"

"No," I said. "No. Nothing's the matter."

I turned and walked away.

22. Boop's was quiet. I sat down and ordered a
beer. There was a Christmas special playing on the television set.

"You okay?" Boop said.

"Yeah, I'm all right."

Porky came in, and I bought him a beer.

"Timmy Lee was lookin' for ya," Porky said. "He says
he'll be over your house tomorrow, wait for him."

"He say where he was?"

"He said he was with some broad, he won't be up. I guess it's the broad he's boffin'."

"Good for him." Boop said. "That's what I call a Christmas present."

"She ain't a bad-looking kid, Boop. You ever see her around here?"

"The kid with the big bazooms? *Marrone,* he's boffin' *her?*"

"Well, if he ain't, I *hope* he is!" Porky said.

"She got some set of *calzones,*" Boop said.

One of the bookmakers came in and Boop poured him a Scotch.

"You glad I didn't get you that thing you were askin' me about?" Porky said.

"I guess I am."

"A kid your age, you don't need trouble. Not that kind of trouble. That's trouble you never get out of."

"I guess you never do."

23.

Timmy came around in the afternoon with the forty dollars. It was Mike who had loaned it to me and I was supposed to pay it out of my first check when I went back to the Navy. We had a beer in Fitzgerald's to celebrate.

"You got any idea where you're going when you go back?" he said.

"I put in for Africa. This place, Port-Lyautey, they have over there."

"A sailor in the desert?"

"Why not?"

He sipped his beer. "You hear from Kathleen?"

"Not a word."

"You're better off."

I had the four tens in my pocket. It was Christmas Eve, deep in the afternoon, and I wanted to get them to my mother.

"I saw your father the other night. He's a pisser."

"He sure is."

I went back to the house. The kids were all there, but my mother was out. I lay down and tried to sleep. And I thought about my father, and how I wanted to talk to him, how I wanted to find out who he was and what he cried about; wanted to tell him about me, describe my hurts and my desires. I wanted to ask him why the Christmas tree meant nothing to him, ask him about his father, and Belfast, and the IRA; get him to talk about my mother, where he met her, when they got married, what they thought a life would be. I was old enough now and tired of the silence. And then, with the kids playing in the hall, I fell into a dreamless sleep.

When I woke up it was after seven, and my mother was sitting alone at the kitchen table, sipping from a cup of hot tea. She was shaking her head slowly.

"I've got some money for you," I said. I laid the four tens on the table.

"Oh, Peter, no, *you'll* need that. We'll manage."

"But you don't have anything for Christmas."

"I've got a few things."

"Come on. You still have time to get to the stores."

And then, very quietly, she started to cry. "Oh, God," she said, "I just wish I could do everything right. I just wonder what God is doing this for."

I didn't know what to do, or how to react; she had always been the strong one in the family, the one who didn't drink and who helped us to survive. I put my hand on her shoulder. She reached up and touched it, kneading it, holding it, touching me.

"Oh, Peter," she said.

I left the money on the table and went out into the night. It was time to drink for the first time in Rattigan's.

24. A light snow was falling, whirled by the wind off the harbor. Rattigan's was like some dark glowing oasis, the muted lights promising warmth. I was still underage and I had not been invited, but it was too late for rules; I was going away in a few days and I wanted to see my father. I wanted to see him in that place where he truly lived, in the place where his personal history beat around him, where everybody had a record of his small wins and his unmentioned losses, the place where he boasted and lied and laughed, and was forgiven everything. I knew now what saloons were for, and why men went there late at night.

I walked across the street, thinking: it would be easier to go up the hill, to go to Midnight Mass and try to find a girl afterwards; to repair to the company of my friends, the sound of Christmas music in my own bars. But I walked into Rattigan's. An unused food counter stood on the right, and an empty refrigerator, both monuments to the noisy days after Prohibition, when the speak-easies closed and Rattigan's had a Chinese cook. Whiskey bottles were piled against the mirror behind the bar, lit up by the Schlitz sign over the cash register. The TV set over the bar was off, but Christmas music was playing on the radio. An instrumental called "Serenata" came out of the old cathedral-shaped box behind the bar. Billy Hamill was sitting on a stool near the entrance to the back room, sipping a beer and talking to some friends. I went right to him.

"Hello, Dad," I said. "Merry Christmas."

He turned, his face surprised. He had three quarters in front of his drink. I put a five on the bar.

"You drinking?" I said.

He hesitated for a moment, looking around him. The other men were talking and drinking.

"Sure. A Budweiser."

George Loftus, the short, wizened bartender, came down the bar. He rubbed the back of his neck. Crosby was singing "Adeste Fideles."

"You're drinkin', Bill?" he said.

"Whatta you think? George, you know Pete, don't you? He's in the Navy now."

"Good ta meet ya, son. What kinda shit ya drinkin'?"

"A Bud. Make it two."

He pulled us two drafts. My father seemed uncomfortable, but he started introducing me around. I remember meeting a huge red-faced cabdriver named John Mullins, a guy named Johnny the Polack, a cop named Joe Whitmore, who had led the investigation of the Collyer Brothers mansion. "This is Peter. My oldest. Home from the Navy." And rough handshakes, and good ta meet ya kid, and how are ya, and it looks like Eisenhower will end the war pretty soon. They would shake my hand and drape an arm around my father and order drinks for the both of us. The place started filling up with men who had been freed from children and Christmas Eve and were looking for some solace.

"Hell, here's Jimmy deGangimi, hey Jimmy, come here, will you, my son's in town, home from the Navy." One old man was playing himself on the shuffleboard machine, cursing at the results, muttering and lost. Near the windows at the far end of the bar there were three guys in their twenties drinking whiskey.

"It's good to see you, Peter," my father said. "Goddammit, I never get to see much of you. You're getting' big, a big kid."

"They feed you pretty good down there."

"The haircut looks good."

"You should've seen me three months ago. I looked like a skinned rat."

He sipped from the beer. "I'm proud of you."

"What for?"

"Servin' your country. You know what I mean."

"It's better than the Army."

"It'll make a man out of you," he said.

I wanted to say a million things and couldn't get any of them out. I guess he couldn't either.

"Did you get your mother anything for Christmas?" he said.

"Not really."

"You should."

"I know."

"She's a wonderful piece of work, your mother."

I sipped the beer.

"Where did you meet her, Dad?"

"What do you mean?"

"I mean, where did you and her meet, you know, before you got married?"

He drained his beer and motioned to George for a refill.

"Ah, Christ, I don't know. A dance, I think. Yeah, a dance. Belfast United. Jesus, those were the days."

"Tell me about them."

"It's too long ago," he said.

"Try."

"Ah hell, you know me." He remembered something. "But Christ, I remember this one dance, I had the wooden leg then, and we all went with some women. There was a guy named Moran, Frankie Moran. I don't think the son of a bitch ever washed in his life. He picks up this woman, and they're on the way to the dance, see, and she begins to smell him, moving away on the subway . . ."

His face started to beam now; something dark had been pushed back, and he was remembering now, old nights, good times.

". . . She says to him, 'Jesus, Frank, your feet smell like hell.' He says, 'Whattaya mean, my feet?' So she tells him again, and says to him she won't be able to get through the night. He promises her he'll buy a pair of new socks as soon as they get off the train, and he does. He goes into a store, buys the socks, puts them on and comes out again. And they go to the dance and one thing leads to another, and she says to him, 'Christ, Frank, it's worse than *ever*.' And he says, the idjit, he says, 'Whatta you mean, I bought new socks. Look,' he says, 'here they are,' and there they were: the dumb bastard was carrying the old pair around in his pocket."

He laughed, and I laughed, and we had another round.

"What was the old country like?"

He looked at me, his eyes wary, and shook his head. "To hell with the old country," he said.

He drained the glass quickly.

"Hit me again, George," he said, sliding the glass a few inches. He looked at me and made an odd little disparaging movement with his hand.

"Ireland . . ."

"I'm serious, Dad. What was it like, when you were, you know, my age?"

"It was a bloody mess."

"Did you kill anyone?"

"What do you mean, kill anybody?"

He looked behind him when he said it, to see where Joe Whitmore was standing. Joe was playing shuffleboard.

"I mean, you were in the IRA."

"I was."

"Well, I thought maybe, well, you might have—"

"Nobody got killed who didn't deserve it."

"You mean the British?"

"Those bastards deserved it."

"What about the priests?"

"Worse," he said.

And then John Mullins was there, and Whitmore was back from the shuffleboard machine, and the music was louder as the bar grew more crowded. The snow was still falling thinly, driven by the wind. They started to talk about guys they knew, someone who had run off, leaving his wife and four kids behind, a beer racket that was going on at Diamond's on New Year's Eve. That son of a bitch O'Malley. The ballplayers oughtta quit. Who the hell does he think he is? They oughtta lock that bastard up. They moved around my father, between me and him, and some of them talked to me, the same questions about the food and the training and where was I going. My father moved among them, laughing, drinking, moving with the flow of the bar. After

a while he came back, and had another one with me. The
beer was getting to him. He reached over and squeezed my
left leg.

"Christ," he said, "I wish I had your legs."

And I loved him in that moment, wanted to put my arm
around him, hold him, tell him that the leg didn't matter,
and being poor didn't matter, none of it mattered. He was
there, still there, he wasn't on relief, he wasn't begging in
subways, he had resisted, he hadn't given up. I touched him,
and then Red Cioffi yelled from down the bar.

"Hey, Billy give us a song!"

My father pointed at the clock. "It's too early, Red."

"Too early, my ass. It's Christmas Eve. Hey, George,
turn that goddamn radio off."

"Maybe Billy don't wanna sing," George said.

"Don't wanna sing, my ass."

George turned the radio off, and my father started to
sing.

> *"Now Mister Patrick McGinty*
> *An Irishman of note.*
> *He fell into a fortune.*
> *And he bought himself a goat."*

"That's the way, Bill," Red yelled. "Go get 'em."

> *" 'A goat's milk,' said Patty,*
> *'I think I'll have me fill.'*
> *But when he got the nanny home—*
> *He found it was a bill."*

The song brought him out of himself and into himself at
the same time, the face shining and young and careless,

alone on the stage. And then song followed song, full of the things I had wanted him to tell me, all the answers there in the texture of the songs, in the lonely somber tone, filled up with exile and anger and longing, all the things he had carried with him across the sea. All the things that came together that Sunday on a winter field in Brooklyn.

> *"Castles are sacked in war*
> *Chieftains are scattered far*
> *Truth is a fixed star!*
> *Eileen, aroon."*

I cheered with the others and hugged him and bought some beers, and he stood there pleased, standing in the gabardine raincoat, and began to sing "Come Back, Patty Reilly."

> *"The boy is a man now,*
> *He's toil-worn, he's tough,*
> *Whispers come over the sea . . ."*

Singing the words, he tipped his glass to me and winked. I joined him at the end.

> *"Oh, come back, Patty Reilly,*
> *To Bally James Duff,*
> *Oh, come back, Patty Reilly, to me."*

The two of us were singing loud, and the regulars cheered and then Red asked for "Galway Bay." We were up to the part where the strangers came and tried to teach us their ways, when one of the younger guys at the other end shouted down the bar, "Hey, knock it off, I can't hear myself t'ink."

The bar went suddenly silent. My father got off his stool, the song snapped shut, and he started down the bar. "Who's the wise guy?" he said. The three guys were laughing now, and one of them said, "Oh, wow, I'm terrified."

That was all my father needed. He went down the bar, limping heavily on the wooden leg, and as the first of the young guys turned, my father pivoted on his good leg, hit him right on the chin with a hook, and the guy went down. The one next to him turned, ready to punch, and I hit him with a right hand, and he went down. The third guy put his hands out, palms forward, placing himself out of it, and the first guy got up, and my father knocked him down again. We were joined there together, my father and I, and we beat them a little more, and then some of the other men came over and shoved them out the door and left them on the sidewalk. My father stared at me for a few long moments, while the life of the bar resumed and people shouted for songs and someone turned on the radio. And then he smiled. I smiled back at him, and we went back to the bar together with our arms around each other.

"Where was I, Magee?"

" 'The strangers came and tried to teach us their ways.' "

Red Cioffi came around the bar and turned off the radio, but before he resumed the song, my father turned to Joe Whitmore and said, "This is my son Peter, in whom I am well proud."

And so we closed the place, drinking into Christmas morning. When we got back upstairs to the kitchen, he showed me what Moore was going to do to Marciano, throwing the short right hand at the lamp cord, the way he used to do it with his friends, when I would lie awake in my bed. "You'll be all right," he said. "You'll be some piece of work." He got up, and put his arm around my neck and hugged me.

"Good night, son," he said. I said good night, and he walked through the apartment to his bedroom, where he undressed slowly in the dark. In the dull light from the street, I could see the bulky pile of freshly wrapped presents lying under the tree. I sat there for a long time, flexing my sore right hand, remembering the frightened face of one of the strangers I had hit for almost nothing a few hours before and the rough ceremony we all had shared. From the darkened rooms, I heard my father toss and then sigh, sounding like a very young boy lost in cruel dreams. I wondered if before he slept, he had touched the ruin of the magic leg.

25. When I went back after Christmas on the bus, there were more soldiers and sailors than before. They talked in the quiet night, about going to Korea and their girls and what they had received for Christmas. I wondered about Sal Costella. I didn't care that much about Brooklyn now, with my girl gone forever and most of my friends in the service, scattering around the country and the world; in some odd way, I felt free, as the bus moved west to Oklahoma and other places, a ride I hoped would take me someday to the Seine. I thought about Audrey Hepburn for a while, and then about North Africa. I hadn't received much for Christmas in any ordinary way; but my father loved me back, and there was no other gift I wanted.

About the Author

PETE HAMILL was born in Brooklyn and served in the Navy. He is a columnist for the *New York Post* and the author of two other books, *Irrational Ravings* and *A Killing for Christ*. He lives in Brooklyn, New York.